The Gorilla's Teeth

The Gorilla's Teeth

Bound by Ritual, Trapped by Fate

Kate Ngozi Nwamadi

EXCELLER BOOKS®
A GLOBAL PRESS

The Gorilla's Teeth
Bound by Ritual, Trapped by Fate

Cover by Exceller Books using resources from Pixabay.com

ISBN: 978-93-48892-75-1

Published in India in 2025 by Exceller Books,
An imprint of GE Group
G1, Dream Apartment, Degree College Road, Belgharia,
Kolkata, 700056, India
www.excellerbooks.com

EXCELLER BOOKS®
A GLOBAL PRESS

Dedication

I dedicate this book to my son, Success Nnaemeka Nwanna, whose unwavering dedication and intentional collaboration have been instrumental in bringing this work to fruition. Son, you have etched your name in the sands of time.

Acknowledgment

I am deeply grateful to the Almighty God for granting me the inspiration and strength to complete this work. My heartfelt thanks go to my husband, Mr. K. C. Nwamadi—this project would not have been possible without you. Thank you so very much.

To my wonderful children, I appreciate your moral support and encouragement throughout the writing process. And again, thank you for typing the manuscript—you guys are truly wonderful. *Mama loves you.*

I extend my sincere appreciation to Prof. (Mrs.) Hope Amolo of the Department of Religion and Peace Studies, Imo State University. Ma, you're one in a million.

To Dr. Primus Ukah, Director of Studies, West Africa Theological Seminary (an affiliate of the University of Nigeria, Nsukka), Owerri Campus—thank you for your numerous forms of support.

Dr. Chibuzor Onuoha, my English lecturer—thank you for doing the first proofreading of this work. Mr. Success Nnaemeka Nwanna—thank you for proofreading it again. Your input is deeply appreciated. You have so much to offer in the writing world.

I acknowledge Dr. Kenneth Butcher, my superior—I have learned a lot from you. Thank you for the good working environment you created for us.

And to Mrs. Osinachi E. Endy Nwaokorie, Lecturer, Department of Humanities, School of General Studies, Federal Polytechnic Nekede, Owerri, Imo State—a leader is always a leader. Thank you for all you do.

Lastly, I express my profound gratitude to my father's house—my parents and siblings—for your unending love and for standing by me in critical times. Indeed, *"Family is all we've got."* I love you all.

Foreword

It is my pleasure to write the forward on this literary masterpiece titled, *'The Gorilla's Teeth: Bound By Ritual, Trapped By Fate'* as authored by Kate N. Nwamadi.

This book, a beautiful work of fiction, captures a twist of fate, from what used to be, to what the present is all about, juxtaposing both the past and the present. From the title, which first captures the attention of anyone who picks it up, to the final chapter, the book wraps one up with a fluid, flowing use of words, transporting the reader into a world of imagination that is effortlessly captured. The rich choice of words, written with simplicity, provides a thoroughly relaxing read that keeps you glued to it from the first page and won't let you put it down until you're done.

The author of the book, a teacher and a songwriter who loves travelling and visiting interesting sites, has obviously drawn inspiration for writing from these activities. It is also clear to see that she is an avid reader which has made her a profound storyteller as can been seen and gleaned from the pages of this beautiful storyline and book which would make it very easy for any reader to connect to and enjoy it and which also puts her in the league of any good storyteller and writer one can think of.

I wholeheartedly recommend this book as a must-read to all lovers of good books with a truly captivating and enjoyable storyline, written to appeal to every class and member of society, while also leaving readers with a glimpse of history.

Prof. Benny U. Ike-Obioha, PhD
HOD, Educational Foundations & Management
Alvan Ikoku Federal University of Education, Owerri.

Contents

Chapter I | Ngba Festival

What excitement is in the air as the people of Aguata prepare for their local festival! It is a competitive festival that is held annually. It has been a way of reunion for several years: reuniting with their sons and daughters in the Diaspora who have been away from home, either because of job or marriage. Usually, the person who becomes victorious in this crucial festive contest will be honoured with a befitting appellation and awarded handsomely with a monetary gift. The loser not only goes home shame-faced but is also meant to give a Billy goat to his opponent, who showed supremacy over him in the competition.

These people were predominantly farmers, and their harvest was usually bountiful each year due to their rich, fertile land and favourable climate conditions. During the festival, there is a kind of aura that comes with it. The people are always happy, knowing fully well that they will make more sales from the visitors who come to watch the fight as they display their healthy and freshly harvested farm produce in their little settlement. It is also a source of pride for any community where the winner emerges. The youths from that village, both male and female, will not allow their neighbouring villages to rest; they will continue to sing, dance, and march around the community in their native outfits, with ecstatic designs all over their bodies, jigging up and down with excitement. It was truly an interesting moment, watching the youth move in their youthful exuberance; nothing could stop them except their own decision to call it a day.

Mazi Ndubueze, one of the title holders from Aguata, popularly known as "Obiagu," and his beautiful wife, Adaobi, who hails from Alaoma—the daughter of Dinta Agbara, a great farmer from Umucheku village in Alaoma community—had been married for seven years without a child. In spite of their predicament, they had been living together in harmony. Mazi Ndubueze was a well-known farmer and employer of labour. He was also very handsome and full of strength. Indeed, nothing was lacking on his farm as far as their normal farm produce was concerned. His wife also gave him maximum support, both in the family and on his farm. People from far and near came to buy from his farm; that notwithstanding, he never missed business on any market day, especially on Eke market days in Igbo land. For him, sitting at home was for lazy people.

Once every year, usually during the harvest period, the farmers from Aguata and some of their family members carried some of their farm produce to Ekeamanno Junction to offer sacrifices and thank the gods for their bountiful harvest. This year, however, there was a change from the usual way the rituals were carried out. The custodian of their oracle, Mazi Nwosu, had told the farmers to prepare alongside their first sons, as they were the only ones who would be at the shrine to perform the annual rituals. The reason for the sudden change was for the gods to choose their next custodian, as Mazi Nwosu was becoming old. The sudden change did not sit well with some of the villagers, especially Mazi Isiukwu, who had also had a bountiful harvest but had lost his son earlier that year to a deadly disease caused by the boy's stubbornness and rebellious spirit. He would not be a part of the ritual because his only surviving children were his three lovely daughters. His wife, on the other hand, lamented, asking the gods why they had brought such misfortune upon them.

One day, as she was praying, she told the gods to do something quickly and take away the shame her son had brought upon her, even if it meant giving her another son before her husband, Isiukwu, decided to take another wife. Actually, there was nothing wrong in their culture with a man taking a second wife, but because of the issues that came with it, many first wives feared their husbands taking another wife and would not opt for it at all. This was not applicable to them alone, as Mazi Obiagu was not left out due to his wife's barrenness.

Adaobi was seated outside on a raffia seat, her head lazily resting on her palm, gazing into nothingness. Her husband's friend, Mazi Okoye, walked in and called her several times, but she did not hear him because she was lost in thought. When he called again, she jumped, startled by his unexpected appearance.

"Nneoma Adaobi," he started, "I did not mean to frighten you but to bring you back to the land of the living, where one can see the beautiful birds with their beautiful colours, both great and small, flying so high and soaring in the atmosphere—the sound that makes me think birds sing as well. What a beautiful sight, seeing some perching on trees, the sun shining so brightly in the sky, eliminating darkness; one could taste the sweet, fresh air, so freshly cooked like my wife's delicious meal. Even the leaves on the trees are moving in the same rhythm as the wind forces them to. Nneoma, take a look at that lovely butterfly. Nature, indeed, is beautiful," he said.

"You have not changed from your funny behaviour," Adaobi retorted. "Don't mind me. As you can see, my husband is not around. I'm thinking about how to fix my bicycle," Adaobi remarked.

Mazi Okoye was perplexed. Looking into the air, he turned around, fastened his eyes on her, and said, "Hmm, Adaobi, since when did you start fixing bicycles? By the way, I inquired about my friend before coming. I'm sure he must be inside. Well, let me call him myself. I am sure you don't know his whereabouts. Obiagu, my friend! Obiagu, where are you?"

"Is that Mazi Okoye?" Obiagu said.

"I knew it! He must be in."

"Of course. Who else did you expect to see?"

Obiagu, coming out from behind his house with a smile, replied, "My good friend, what other jackpot did you win this time? I can see the excitement on your face. This can't be ordinary!"

"Obiagu, my friend, a handshake will suffice." They shook hands and exchanged pleasantries.

"Eyim. Well, I've come to tell you how it went at the Ekeamanno Junction."

Obiagu replied, "Will it be of any good to me since my family was not represented? Since the gods have refused to give me a child, I have a lot of food and money in my house. Raising children wouldn't have been a problem. Even my ancestors are quiet about this matter. Do they want me to go to the grave without someone to carry on the family lineage?"

"Obiagu, my friend, I know you are kind-hearted and strong. Don't worry—one day, this challenge will be a thing of the past."

Obiagu looked away, staring at the clouds as if he were looking at his ancestors. Only he truly knew what he was thinking. In a jiffy, his countenance changed, and he replied to his friend, Okoye, in a gentle and soothing manner,

"I hope so. I really hope so."

"Yes, that's the spirit," Okoye said, but quickly added, "All the same, I will still give you my gist. It won't hurt. As you know, many awful things were performed, usually in secrecy. Even sacrifices were offered before coming to the junction. Not everyone was allowed to witness it for reasons I do not know. If you asked, they would tell you it was for great minds. Anyway, that's beside the point. At the junction, after all was said and done, Mazi Nwosu performed some rituals, followed by the libation, to welcome the spirits of the dead—our ancestors—to be part of the sacrifice."

With a voice smeared with curiosity, Obiagu asked, "After that, what happened?"

"Of course, there was jubilation everywhere because the chief priest gave his announcement that the goddess of the land, *Ala*, was pleased with the sacrifice," Mazi Okoye said.

"After that, what again?" Obiagu persisted.

"Yes, my friend, that was the climax of the whole thing. We were asked to assemble our sons, who were dressed in our native attire with white chalk lining their bodies as they walked around the shrine after much incantation and consultation by the chief priest. It was like a dream to me. In fact, I have not come out of that ecstasy. Eventually, my son Ikenna was chosen by the gods. I can't believe this!" he said, lifting his hands in the air and turning around frantically with joy. In his heart, this showed that the gods had been favourable to him.

"You've been a very lucky man," Obiagu said. "The gods have blessed you with children—not just any kind of children, but three promising sons, firmly planted like the iroko tree. Your farm is doing well, and not just that, you have many economic trees that you inherited from your father. And now, your first son, Ikenna, is going to be the next custodian of our oracle, *Anya Ugo*—the eyes of the people and the mouthpiece of the gods. Our own Ikenna, that little boy of yesterday!" he added.

"I am happy for you. Okoye, my friend, look at me. I, Obiagu, had a bountiful harvest, too, but I have no son to go with me to the Ekeamanno Junction. My friend, just go to my barn and take as much yam as you want. Go to my pen and take any size of goat that appeals to your eyes. It is my way of expressing my joy for your son's election. I am happy for you, *nnam*," Obiagu remarked.

Okoye replied, "My good friend, I know you can do anything for me. I really appreciate it." And in a split second, his countenance changed. "But Obiagu, my friend, I am worried about your family too. If it were a matter of strength, you would have had more sons than I do. I remember that no one has ever fought with you and won the battle. You are the pride of our community, the man who holds the highest title in our land, the emblem of strength, and the only man who wears the head of a lion as an ornament. But you can see, my friend, that this present situation does not require physical strength but wisdom. What did I say?" Mazi Okoye placed more emphasis on this by gently pulling his ear and looking straight into his eyes. "Be wise!"

Mazi Obiagu just stared motionlessly at him.

Mazi Okoye continued, "I remember vividly that my father, Diokpa, told you, Obiagu, to marry from the same village where my wife hails from, but you did not listen. Was it because he was not your biological father? As a friend, I told you to take another wife, but you did not heed my precious advice. Now, I'll suggest that you visit a spiritualist if you don't mind. This time around, I hope you don't throw down my suggestion like you did previously."

"You may be right," said Obiagu, "but on the issue of a second wife, *COUNT ME OUT!* I don't want to hurt my wife.

She has been obedient and loving. Well, I'll see how I can discuss it with her. Thanks."

"Alright! I'll be on my way, my good friend."

"Lezie anya!"

Chapter 2 | Aguata Women's Meeting

One eke market is gone, yet Mazi Obiagu does not know how to relate what Mazi Okoye told him to his wife. Before the next eke market, he bought new wrappers, jewellery, and shoes for his lovely wife to make her happy. The following day, he purchased freshwater fish and asked her to prepare a special pepper soup for them to enjoy.

-At the table-

"Nneoma, this pepper soup is delicious. Goodness me! Every ingredient in it is perfectly blended. Thank God you did not spice it with too much pepper, as I always asked you to. I must say, my love, this is the sweetest I've had recently." Obi's eyes glittered like a nine-year-old's while he wolfed down the delicacy before him.

"Ehhh, Obim, so you go about tasting pepper soup from different joints, eh?" She looked at him with a feigned scowl as she inquired.

"No, no! Nneoma, that is not what I do, ohh. All I was just trying to say is that you're the best cook!"

"Nna Anyi, are you serious?" she asked gleefully while carrying used dishes from the ground to the other end of the room.

"You think I'm lying about you being the best cook? Okay, fine, were you not at Ofoma's daughter's traditional wedding ceremony? Did you not see the kind of food that was served there? The whole thing was over-spiced, and nobody enjoyed the meal. The food was so peppery that we were all begging for water, and the available water wasn't enough. If it were possible, we would have run to a nearby river just to quench our thirst and calm down the hotness of the pepper. If you were hired as a caterer for that occasion, we wouldn't have gone through all we did at that traditional wedding. You would have shown them how wonderful you are in the kitchen."

"Nnanyi, it's okay; now you are making my head swell," she said with love shimmering in her eyes.

Mazi Obiagu added, "My love, oh, let the head swell. I'm telling you the truth, and I know that now you are happy with me, so instead of wasting my time eating that tasteless pepper soup some people cook outside, I'd rather stick to my wife's pepper soup, where everything blends perfectly—just like her lovely face. Come, let me touch it a little."

"Nnanyi Ibiakwa, you will not leave me alone now! I know you are driving at something. Just let me go; you will not get me with your old trick."

Mazi Obiagu licked his lips humorously and started, "Not at all, Oriaku'm, but we will get there soon! Of all the women that were paraded before me in this community, you were the only one that appealed to my heart."

"Eh, nnanyi, did I hear you well? What about that girl at Ofoma's daughter's traditional wedding, whom your eyes were glued to? You almost forgot that I was seated next to you!"

"My love, please forgive me. Sometimes, our eyes wander away." That does not establish the fact that I don't love you. Let me tell you once again that I love you more than anything in the world. Remember the first time I met you? I told you that I love you more than my—"

"Please, Obim, don't let her spirit hear this," she cut in immediately. "No man can love you more than his mom. It's just one of the ways you men use to deceive women and make us fall as cheap prey into your hands." She said this with feigned contempt, then her countenance became moody, and she hung her shoulders and started, "Nnanyi, I want to use this opportunity to thank you once again for the things you bought for me the other day. And I'm equally sorry for not bearing children for you."

Her husband interrupted, "Don't let this bother you, my dear. It is not your fault, and I believe the gods will grant our request one day. That reminds me of a friend of mine, Mazi Okoye, whom you are acquainted with and who offered to help us out. He told me of a spiritualist who can be of help to us. What do you think about that?"

"Nnanyi, we can give it a try; at least we have waited long enough."

Fortnightly, every afor is always the meeting day for the women in Aguata. They consider it a special day because they see it as a day of rest. The following afor, in the evening, the women gathered at the home of their leader, the usual place for their meeting. The minutes of the last meeting were read, adopted by Nneoma Chinwendu, and supported by Uloma, the Provost. Nneoma Adaobi Ndubueze, who arrived late to the meeting and did not understand their deliberation, demanded that the minutes be read for clarification. She was interrupted by Chiawuotu, the secretary.

"Who, me, read it again? Hiyakwa! Madam, look at me; I'm a very busy woman. What exactly kept you at home?" She stretched out her hands and gestured, "Look at us, busy women who are occupied with different activities at home and still made it early to the meeting."

"Excuse me! Is there anything wrong with rereading it? Or has it now become a crime to read the minutes twice?" Nneoma asked indignantly.

"Yes, Nneoma Adaobi, yes. Everything is wrong with reading it again for a childless woman like you, who has nothing—apparently nothing—to do at home but just decided to come late to the meeting to hear what able mothers like us would say. If I may ask, was it your son or daughter that kept you at home, or was it that impotent husband of yours?"

Gasps escaped the crowd. Her eyes conveyed hate, and her voice reeked of contempt. Those words dug deep into Nneoma's soul and shattered it into a thousand pieces. She looked around with pleading eyes, but no one maintained eye contact or broke composure. No one came to her rescue.

"Oh my God! Chiawuotu, has it come to this? Is it my fault that I don't have any children yet?" she said, trying not to choke on incoming tears. "Well, I'm leaving, and my husband must hear this." She started to stand up, wanting to get as far away from there as possible, but Chiawuotu was ready for her.

"Ha, ha, ha! Did I hear you say 'husband'?" Chiawuotu said sarcastically, clapping her hands in contempt.

"Shut up, Chiawuotu!" the chairlady interrupted. "What has come over you? Are you taking this matter personally, or do you have some scores to settle with her? Even if you do, you must maintain decorum here. As an executive member, you know our rules. However, let me ask the women what the right thing to do is." She scanned around calmly for a willing candidate.

Mmawanyi raised her hand.

"Yes, you! What do you have to say? Speak as the women's leader."

Mmawanyi replied, "Our constitution states that after a case is deliberated upon, the offender will be fined as follows: a jar of palm wine, two plates of oil beans with okporoko, and one live chicken—not without an apology."

"Does anyone else have something to say?" asked the Provost.

Two women raised their hands.

"Okay, you, Obidiya, let's hear you."

"Eh, bikonuoooo, there is nothing to deliberate upon. The case is clear, and Chiawuotu is to be fined. Thank you!" she said and took her seat.

"Hmm, supporters club. So you are on the side of Nneoma Adaobi? Anyway, it is not your fault. Look at that lazy goat that does not even have the strength to farm, and that stupid man married her just because of her colour—pawpaw, ocha ka make. She doesn't even know her left from her right. Why won't you support her? Mad woman! Birds of the same feather always flock together!" Chiawuotu spat and made a nasty sound with her mouth as she took her seat angrily while her own flock of supporters approved in muffled tones.

"Enough!" Uloma yelled at Chiawuotu.

"Order, both of you! This very minute!" the Provost reprimanded. "All we want is peace and not trouble." She turned to the rest of the women. "If you have any issues at home, resolve them before coming here so you don't transfer aggression onto innocent people. I don't understand what is going on here today! What is going on?" Uloma inquired, looking around as if really expecting an answer.

Finally, Nneoma left the meeting with a heavy heart. On getting home, she saw her husband resting under a mango tree that was about to bud, with both hands crossed over his chest. She walked straight to him. Noticing another presence in his midst, he lifted his head up slightly and was taken aback.

"Ah ah! Nneoma, you are back so soon! Did the meeting not hold?" One could hear the concern in his voice. Nneoma, whose eyes were filled with tears, burst out crying, leaving her husband puzzled.

"What is it? What happened?" Placing his hand around her shoulder, he asked again. "Did you receive any bad news today? Please calm down and talk to me, Adaobimu, inugo?"

Nneoma Adaobi slowly placed her head on his chest and narrated the whole story to him, leaving him disconcerted.

"Nneoma, you see, this is one of the reasons we must go and see the spiritualist as soon as possible. Things are really getting out of hand. However, cheer up, my dear. It is one of those things that can happen to a man. But, my dear, I promise you that we must go and see Chiawuotu's husband. As a matter of fact, let's go now while the case is still hot. What nonsense! Which marital right did I not fulfil when I came to marry you? Or did anyone tell them that I, Obiagu, owe your parents a dime? As a matter of fact, I gave more than what they asked for. Then why would any woman on earth treat you like a piece of trash? This woman has let the lion out of its den."

-At Chiawuotu's house-

Knock, knock, knock.

"Who is it again? Please, come in. Oh, it's you, Mazi Obiagu, with your wife. Did she not attend the meeting? My wife is not back yet," he added.

"Mazi Egbule, she did attend the meeting but returned quite early."

"Why did she return early when they haven't closed the meeting? Besides, this is their last meeting for the year, and it's usually characterized by different local dishes. I am salivating already! I know that my wife will bring some for me. Or is anything wrong?" His eyes darted from Mazi Obiagu's face to his wife's.

"That is the reason we're here. You see, Mazi Egbule, I was surprised when I saw my wife in tears. She told me how your wife insulted her at the meeting. We have learned the reason for all the insults and name-calling."

"Mazi Obiagu, you've done well, and as you can see, my wife is not home yet. So, what can I offer you before she comes back?"

"Don't worry. We are not hungry."

After about 15 minutes, Chiawuotu returned home. She saw her guests, threw in a greeting, and walked straight into the room. Her husband followed behind to tell her why their guests were waiting. Furious, she dashed out of the room and began scolding Nneoma in the presence of her husband.

"Adaobi, is it because of the little thing that happened at the meeting that you've come to spoil my name before my husband? Do you want to kill my husband for me? Is he a woman that you're complaining to him? Oh, you want to show me that you have a husband whom you can move like a piece of cloth, and I don't have any?"

Chiawuotu's husband was startled, exhaled deeply, and, with anger on his face, said, "So, Chiawuotu, what they said about you is true? Thank God I did not defend you before you came back, oh! Who in this village does not know that Adaobi is not a troublesome woman? Anyone claiming otherwise must be mad or living in absolute solitude. Chiawuotu, be careful and stop spoiling my good name in this village." He pointed at her with a shaky finger, writhing with rage.

"Bia, Egbule, if you don't know what to say, you can as well keep quiet and let me address the situation. Your fellow man came over to our house to beat me up, and you're here supporting them. By the way, what good name do you want to protect? Shameless man!"

Mazi Egbule pleaded with Adaobi and her husband not to be angry at his wife's misbehaviour. Obiagu replied, "My dear, what else can I say? We've seen how you're living with fire in your house. This woman is hell. Goodness me! I can't put up with this ill-mannered woman. She sounds like a deadly disease. Also, tame your dog, or someone else will do it for you. Please, let's leave before I lose my temper. She is getting me irritated."

Chiawuotu broke in indifferently, "Ha, ha, ha! If you like, go or stay. I can only withdraw my words when I see Adaobi carrying a child. Shameless woman with her shameless husband! I can see that you both have gone mad, and you should thank your lucky stars that I'm in a good mood. If I had woken up on the wrong side of the bed, you would have seen my wrath! I would have poured very hot soup on both of you so you would go blind and wouldn't be able to complain to my husband or even come close to my house again."

Egbule shouted, "Abomination!! Chiawuotu, you must follow this family home and apologize to them! If you refuse, I'll cease to eat your food from henceforth!"

"I won't, Nnanyi! If you like, don't eat. The food wouldn't even be enough for the children and me."

"Chiawuotu, you don't understand. I said I won't eat your food again if you don't go and apologize to them, and it won't just stop at that. I will stop giving you money as well. That means I don't need you anymore. I can't believe that you are the woman I used my hard-earned money to marry. You are a disgrace to womanhood!"

Egbule said these words angrily and walked away. You should have seen how furious he was—it made him shout like he was going insane. Even his domestic animals went into hiding. The stern Chiawuotu was terrified by her husband's reaction. She had no other option but to vamoose from his presence.

As she was leaving, she cried out, "Eh, Nnanyi, I'm sorry, oh! I can't go through all this, oh! I thought I had you all wrapped around my finger. You know me, Nnanyi, you know that I cannot do without money. That means my mother will also suffer from this. Okay, I am sorry, oh! In fact, Nnanyi, I'm on my way to their house to make the apology official. Please, I'm on my knees!" She ran after him, gripping his clothes from behind while simultaneously trying to kneel.

Chapter 3 | The Visit to Aguba Shrine

Mazi Obiagu and his wife, Adaobi, approached Mazi Okoye's home. On seeing them from afar, he welcomes them and asks, "My father of blessed memory told me that the toad does not run in the daytime just for the sake of running—either something is after it, or it is running after something. Hence, what brings you to my house this hot afternoon?"

"Actually, my friend, you got it completely right," Mazi Obiagu said. "I have discussed what you told me about the other day with my beautiful wife, and we have decided to give your suggestion a trial."

Mazi Okoye nodded approvingly. "Now you are talking. I was with the Chief Priest yesterday, and he told me he'd be travelling to Okposi to get some items needed to perform some sacrifices for his customers. He also told me that if the items are not complete, he will proceed to Abiam until they are."

"So what are you suggesting?" Obiagu asked.

"We are going to give him at least three market days before going to see him," said Okoye. "That reminds me, what can I offer you?"

"As usual, you can ask my wife." He gestured lightly at his wife.

"No need. I know she will like the anu nchi with palm wine as well. Ha ha ha!" Mazi Okoye said in between chuckles.

"My friend, you can say that again. Just hold on, let me call my wife. Ijeoma! Ijeoma!"

Four market days later, Mazi Okoye, Mazi Obiagu, and his wife, Adaobi, set out to go to the spiritualist's shrine. The place was barricaded with dozens of bamboo sticks adorned with skulls of humans and baboons. The red and white materials situated around the place aggravated Adaobi's fear. Mazi Obiagu noticed her panicked state and interlocked his fingers with hers to make her feel safe.

The shaman sat on the floor, streaks of white and black uli running from his temple all the way down to his jaw, making him appear even more sinister. There were more streaks on his burly body.

Mazi Okoye started, "Greetings, a great one. I'm sure you remember the conversation we had the other time."

"Yes, I do."

"So, how did it go? Were you able to get all the items needed?"

"Yes, I did get them, except for one vital item. Thanks for asking. Who are those with you?"

"Oh, my friend and his wife. They have come to seek a solution to their problem."

"Ok, you are familiar with the shrine. Go back and sit with them right there. You also know that this shrine is quite dreaded—people don't misbehave here. Have you told them that?" He spoke with a reserved yet powerful tone.

"Yes, Udenne."

"Then let me go and consult the oracle, and when I'm done, bring them in the normal way. Of course, you are not a stranger here. Very soon, we shall be working together."

He started singing incantations while juggling items one could barely identify—shells, coloured pebbles, dishevelled carcasses of little rodents, and human teeth. He then set aside eight stones and shared them in twos, representing the four market days: Eke, Orie, Afor, and Nkwo.

Udenne fe nelu ofeda ani
Udenne fe nelu ofeda ani
Udenne fe nelu ofeda ani
Udenne feda ni oburu ihe ochoro
Udenne kedi ihie kpatara indija aba

After several minutes of chanting, bobbing his head, and glancing around as if seeing spirits hovering in the air, he looked at them.

"You and your wife have been childless for almost eight years now, and you have come to seek a solution. I know you would have preferred a baby boy to carry on your family name, but the gods want to give you a baby girl. Remember, there must be a price to pay; of course, you know nothing goes for nothing. In your case, the gods have asked you to get all the materials needed for your job. Here is the list of what to buy. You can leave now and come back when the items are complete."

Mazi Obiagu, or Okoye, his friend, was not careful while asking about the price.

They trudged the bushy path leading back to their home.

"Where on earth am I supposed to get these items?" Obiagu demanded.

"Don't worry, my friend. It is not an easy task. Try your best to get the ones you can. I can help you with some," Okoye said reassuringly.

One week had gone by. Mazi Obiagu had gone to the market he was familiar with, yet the items were still not ready. Four days later, his friend Okoye visited him to see how far he had gone. He met his absence, but his wife, Adaobi, was home alone.

While he was chewing the kola presented to him by Adaobi, Obiagu, her husband, walked in.

"Okoye!" shouted Obiagu. "I was just thinking of coming over to your place to see you, and—"

He was interrupted by Okoye. "My friend, have you got all the items?"

Obiagu replied, "I've gone around the markets that I know of, yet the items are nowhere to be found." One could hear the despair in his voice.

Okoye laughed heartily. "Ha, ha, ha! With this little brain of yours, do you really think you can get everything in the open market? Just follow me, and I will show you where! It is getting dark, though this is the best time to get some of these things."

Obiagu followed him immediately, and his wife beckoned to him. "Nna, please stay back and have something. You left home in the morning, and I know you must be hungry by now. I have prepared your favourite food."

"It's like you read my mind. I don't know what I would do without you." Obiagu glanced at his wife admiringly and added, "You are the best!" He turned to Okoye. "Please, Okoye, join me."

-At the table-

"Please, come and join me and eat since you didn't hear me the first time."

"Ah ah! You don't have to invite me. I had already made up my mind to join you when I heard your wife call the food your 'favourite.' I knew it must be something very, very delicious. I want my stomach to be as big as yours."

He cupped his belly and pranced around dramatically, trying to imitate Obiagu. They burst out in uproarious laughter.

"Okoye, you amaze me," Obiagu said between stifled chuckles. "People say that my size is not ideal for a man or, in fact, for anyone. But if it is because of the food, expect me at your place tomorrow because I know that your favourite food will make me trim down like you," Obiagu said.

"Ha, ha, ha! There he goes again. Just say that you want to come and eat back the portion of food I'm eating in your house now. If I had known, I would have measured it to give you back the same size."

Then Okoye stopped mid-conversation and glanced out the window with keen eyes. Then he pointed. "My friend, look at that bird on that ube tree! Look at its colour! I don't even know where these birds are migrating from."

"Where?!" Obiagu lit up with curiosity. "I do not see anything. Are you even—"

He glanced back at the table to see Okoye cramming his piece of meat down his throat.

"Okoye, you deceived me! There was never a colourful bird! You only created a diversion in a bid to have my meat, you cunning tortoise!"

As they were trudging deeper into the forest, Obiagu shouted, "Okoye, where are you taking me to? I have never walked in a thick forest like this before."

"Don't worry, we will get there soon. Look straight over there; can't you see those people moving around? All these people have one problem or another; you are not the only one with a problem. This man will provide what you cannot find around our vicinity. Take, for instance, the egg of a python—where on earth do you think one could get it from? But he has it."

"If I may ask, who is this man?"

"I don't really know him, oh. It was a friend of mine who brought me to him when life wanted to knock the wind out of me. I had a life-threatening issue; it was a horrible situation, and help was coming from nowhere. There was practically air around me, but I was choking. I was standing on a hard surface, but I was sinking. My friend, you wouldn't understand until you are in such a situation, but I don't want you to get there. That is why I have decided to stand by you and help you. Actually, this place is always quiet as the graveyard, I must tell you. All I see people do is give him the list of what they want; he provides for them and collects his money.

"Obiagu, if you are courageous enough, you can ask him his name, his father's name, and possibly his place of birth—maybe he is from your maternal home."

"If you are curious, why don't you just ask him yourself? What am I going to do with his name?" Obiagu questioned. "Just hurry up, and let's leave here."

"You're scared already?"

"Yes, I am! Please, hurry up so we can vamoose," he said while eyeing the lot nervously.

"Look at you! Thank goodness we have a clement weather. The last time I came here, it was actually windy. You needed to see how these trees, which you are looking at as if they don't have strength in them, were moving—kissing each other like nothing else. If not, because what I came looking for was paramount, I would have zoomed off. Nevertheless, I endured like a brave man."

Obiagu was indifferent to Okoye's tales and instead worried about his own safety.

Chapter 4 | At Osina River

Obiagu arrived at Udenne's shrine with the complete items. Udenne made some incantations and told him the steps he would take to purify himself and his wife before the sacrifice.

"You may leave now and come back after four market days at the Osina River, where the rituals are to be carried out," Udenne said to Obiagu, Adaobi's husband. "All you have to do is watch me bathe your wife and apply all these on her. However, I will not hesitate to do anything else the gods want me to do to her in the process. Just to clarify, these rituals must be performed by me, Udenne. You must not touch her. Don't even try to stop me until after eight weeks. You may leave now and bring her back after five days for the sacrifice."

Obiagu flashed an indignant look as if trying to object. He immediately glanced at his wife upon hearing Udenne's words. She had wrapped her arms around herself defensively. Obiagu was writhing with anguish, but he stayed mute. He was smart enough to know that it was the only way.

Five days later, at exactly 12 noon, they were at Osina River to perform the rituals. Udenne's voice cut powerfully through the splashes of the serene river.

"It is your duty to bring out all the items for the sacrifice from the basket, Obiagu." Then he turned to Adaobi, "Woman! Remove your dress, tie this white wrapper, and look into the river. Do not hold a thought in your mind; allow the serenity of the river to envelope you. If you begin to feel dizzy, let me know."

He turned back to Obiagu. "Look at the items again. Are they exactly what you brought?"

"Yes, wise one, they are," Obiagu said, his eyes thoroughly fixated on the items right in front of him.

"Woman, how are you feeling now?"

"Wi…Wise one," Adaobi stuttered, "I am so tired, abnormally tired… like I could fall into the river right now."

"Good. This is the moment I've been waiting for. Obiagu, come closer, repeat after me, and throw the items one after the other into the river."

Obiagu obeyed without hesitation. Udenne made some incantations over them and then handed the white wrapper worn by Adaobi to her, instructing her to drape it on her bed and leave it there until after her conception. After conception, they were to burn the white wrapper and pour the ashes back into the river.

Two months later, Nneoma Adaobi unbelievably had a baby bump. Boundless joy filled their hearts. News of Adaobi's pregnancy spread fast like wildfire. Everyone, especially the women, came in numbers to confirm the news. Most women who had once spat on her began to develop a change of attitude toward her.

Her well-wishers showered her and her unborn child with amazing gifts. Adaobi and her husband completed the latter part of the ritual as directed by the chief priest. The pregnancy developed very well without any complications. Nine months later, a healthy, beautiful baby girl was born. As usual, the news of Adaobi's delivery was the talk of the village. Mazi Okoye was the first to bring his gift items to the family, and several others followed.

Like every normal child, she was breastfed and drank water from the same river as others. She was trained to sit, crawl, and walk and was named Nmirioma. She lacked nothing, as her father had vowed to do all he could to give her a proper upbringing, no matter the cost. Nmirioma grew into a lovely and hardworking girl, loved by all. When she came of age, her father did not hesitate to send her to Ota Akara School. Nmirioma was doing well both at home and in school, and joy never ceased in their home.

When Nmirioma was ten years old, her mother took her along to buy some freshwater fish by the riverbank. Her husband, Mazi Obiagu, was a lover of fresh fish pepper soup. As Adaobi was bargaining, Nmirioma snuck away further toward the river, leaving her mother unaware.

Immediately, as she stepped into the river, she felt a strange sensation, like a ripple of energy ascending from the sea and surging through her body with an uncanny force. She attempted to scream, but it was futile because she could not open her mouth. After a few seconds, she fainted.

Meanwhile, intense fear rippled through Adaobi when she noticed her daughter was no longer beside her. She quickly raised the alarm, and Nmirioma was found by the riverbank. Her mother was bewildered, as she had no idea what had happened.

Unknown to Adaobi, the river goddess had sensed Nmirioma's energy and immediately possessed her when she made contact with the river. After several minutes of trying to resuscitate her, Nmirioma coughed out water and involuntarily reached for her mother.

"Wow! She's alive."

"Thank goodness, she is alive!" the crowd chanted.

As soon as they got home, Adaobi narrated the incident to her husband. Mazi Obiagu did not see anything wrong with what had happened.

"Well, I guess she was overwhelmed by the large body of water. You know it's far mightier than our village stream. Or perhaps she has not yet mastered the art of swimming. It could happen to anyone, but we thank the universe for her life," Mazi Okoye said.

Three months later, Nmirioma, the lovely and obedient girl, turned into something else. She became a thorn in the flesh of her family members and everyone around her. She fought with everyone and everything. At school, she was no better—she insulted her fellow students and even the teachers. Her parents were at a loss because the complaints were becoming unbearable.

Nmirioma began to appear and disappear. On one occasion, she vanished into thin air, and all efforts to locate her proved abortive. She was found two days later by the riverbank. When questioned by her parents about what she was doing there, all she could say was, "I want to go home. Take me home."

Her mother was perplexed. "We are here to take you home. Which other home are you talking about?"

Mazi Obiagu, who could no longer cope with the unsettling situation, went to see his friend, Mazi Okoye. He narrated the incident to him, and Okoye was surprised and dumbfounded at the latest development. All he could do was involuntarily nod his head and tap his foot. He was lost in thought.

"You mean she did all these?"

"Exactly! Even more," Obiagu said.

"Just yesterday, when the elders were at my place having a meeting, she poured sand into their palm wine and nkwobi, which my wife had prepared for them. None of the elders took a sip or a bite except Nze Amemechi, who, in spite of the sand, ate and drank as if the sand was a catalyst in the food!"

"Ha, ha, ha! That man never ceases to amaze me. So you mean he hasn't cut down on his gluttony?"

"My friend, you heard me well. He ate sumptuously."

"In that case, we must do something about him before he brings disgrace to the council of elders. But that's by the way. So, what are we going to do about your daughter's case? I think it's high time we saw Udenne," Okoye said.

"Udenne? For what? I have no other business with him," Obiagu retorted reproachfully.

"You never can tell, man!" Okoye replied.

Chapter 5 | At the Grave Side

As agreed, they went to see Udenne at his shrine. While they trudged along the bushy pathway, they spotted a figure from afar—it was Udenne. He was standing akimbo in front of his shrine as if expecting them. When they came closer, they noticed he was clad in his native Isiagu sleeveless top and his usual black khaki shorts. His legs looked like they were made out of interwoven tree roots; he was sturdy and strong. There wasn't a glitter in his eyes when he saw them, even though it had been a couple of years. Instead, he kept chewing fervently on a stick and looking far off into the distance.

"Ah, what brings you to my shrine after so many years?" he asked. Before anyone could reply, he continued, "You thought you would never return? Don't you know that nothing goes for nothing?"

"Nothing goes for nothing?" Obiagu echoed Udenne's words, which made him plunge into deep thought. He knew Udenne had made such a statement before. "What... do you mean by that?"

"Ha ha ha! You requested an overwhelmingly big favour, one that burgeons beyond our reality and requires mystical intervention, and you never bothered to ask for the spiritual repercussions because you were desperate. This question of yours comes too late, but anyway, I'll give you an answer. Some years back, after the birth of your daughter, you were meant to bring me some token of appreciation—a sacrifice—a nanny goat to the spirits before giving your child a name."

They exchanged confused glances and muttered anxiously among themselves. When Udenne observed they had nothing to say, he heaved a sigh and continued.

"As you know, years have gone by, and things are not the same. So I'll have to consult my oracle first to know what next to do." He turned around and started making his way into the shrine. When he had gone a few inches past the entrance, he stopped and glanced behind with a stern look as if to say, ***"I hope you both still remember the traditional way to enter the shrine."***

Obiagu acted accordingly, and his friend followed suit.

Udenne performed some incantations, but he received no answers from the gods. All his calls fell on deaf ears. He tried and tried but to no avail. Finally, he told them what the problem was—that the gods were angry with them, and they would have to leave and come back in four days' time with the following items: a cock, two snakes' eggs, and a white bird not more than a month old. He warned them not to make any mistakes because they must appease the gods.

On the fourth day, Obiagu and his friend returned to the Chief Priest with the required items. The sacrifice was done, and finally, the spirits answered.

"The gods have answered. They have heard your cry and accepted the sacrifice, but one of them is yet to be appeased. You have another sacrifice to make to the goddess of the river. And let me remind you that it's difficult to appease her because her task is always difficult."

"Your honour, we are so far into the journey that turning our backs at this point would be foolish. We have to go through until the end. Whatever the goddess wants, we will bring," Obiagu said.

Udenne blinked. Not a speck of emotion could be spotted on his face. Without any pep talk, he unapologetically said, "She demands your grandmother's teeth."

Obiagu's heart escaped into his belly. Okoye jumped.

"Not just a tooth. The entire set," Udenne added.

"Ah!" escaped Okoye's throat.

"Bu…but? What do you mean by my grandmother's teeth? Where and how am I supposed to get that?" Obiagu demanded pleadingly. "Are you aware that my grandmother is dead? She passed on over 14 years ago. So tell me, how am I going to make that happen? I mean, where do I start?"

"Yes, kind sir. She has been dead for more than a decade. It would be a wild goose chase to extract a tooth, just one o, let alone the whole set," Okoye added.

"Obiagu, listen. I told you before now that the goddess of the river is very difficult to appease because of the kind of task she assigns. But be warned, she wants the complete set of her teeth, which includes her canines, incisors, molars, and premolars. You either get these, or you lose your daughter forever!"

"My God! This is impossible!" Okoye interjected.

"What do I do? Where do I start? My God!" Obiagu involuntarily placed his palms on his head and walked to and fro. He turned back to Udenne, who stared motionlessly at them. When Obiagu saw no hope from Udenne, he turned to Okoye, gripped his shirt, and continued hysterically, "I thought you were trying to help me out! What will I tell my wife?"

"Obiagu, get a hold of yourself!" Okoye reprimanded. "Wasn't the problem solved? You sure do have a child now, don't you? Why are you trying to blame me? I was only trying to help you out!"

"Silence!" The Chief Priest cut in before Obiagu could retaliate. "Silence! Before I turn both of you into two-nosed jackals. For your information, you have just four days to get it. Now, leave before you disturb the solitude of the gods and aggravate them further." With outstretched hands, he resumed his incantations.

"Grandma's teeth? The full set?" Obiagu pondered aloud while they walked through the pathway leading back to their residence. "Never in my life have I ever seen a man given such an impossible task. I must be the first! Why me?!"

A pigeon flew past, situated itself on a branch overhead, and gazed at them keenly as if to empathize with their predicament.

"My brain cells have been split into a thousand bits from pondering on what to do. How to get it? Do you remember where your grandmother was buried? Did she die a bad death, and was her body thrown into an evil forest where wild beasts devoured her carcass?"

Obiagu stared at Okoye in utter disbelief.

"Why are you staring at me as if my ears are morphing into tentacles?"

"Was it not before our very eyes that her remains were buried in her small hut? Okoye, countless times I have told you to turn down your intake of snuff a tad bit. It is causing your memory loss."

"It is you who is becoming amnesiac," Okoye said indignantly, pointing at Obiagu with contempt. "You forget that it's been several years! A lot has happened since then!"

"But... wait... wait," Obiagu interrupted. "Who do you think will allow you to open up the grave?"

"Is that your problem?" Okoye asked. "Don't worry, we will go in the middle of the night."

"Alright, but what am I going to tell my wife?"

"Obiagu, if not for our friendship, I would have totally ignored this hilarious question you asked. Are you not the man of your house—an entity that stands to urinate? You can do whatever pleases you. Are you not the one that married her with your money, I mean your hard-earned money? You're free to tell her whatever pleases you. Tell her anything. In fact, you could even tell her that you want to harvest money from the buttocks of a hippopotamus, and she will not flinch."

Obiagu scowled at Okoye.

"Why do you joke all the time, even in critical situations? Sometimes, I try my best to take you seriously, but it is not easy, I tell you."

Okoye chuckled.

"My friend, my friend. At this point, I can't proceed any further. You know this junction is closer to my home, and I walked this distance just to accompany you. Remember, you've been given just four days. Godspeed, friend." And then he started toward the direction of his house.

Obiagu dragged himself home, his muscles heavy with confusion and despair.

-At Obiagu's Residence-

"Obimu," Adaobi, who was wearing a red flower-patterned wrapper and a black scarf laced around her head, ran eagerly to her man and wrapped her arms around him. "You are welcome. You look famished and unhappy. Did anything go wrong today?"

"No, my dear. It's just that I walked a really long distance. Give me water to drink; I will be fine. Where is Nmirioma?"

"Oh! She is not home."

Two days had passed, and the task of extracting the teeth was fruitless. Mazi Okoye went to see his friend Obiagu and said to him, "We must make it tonight."

"Yes, Okoye, I don't want to be turned into an evil bird. I have never done such a thing in my life before. Are you sure that we are going to make it out alive? Last night, I was startled to death by all the scary noises I heard—my heart was almost out of me."

"You sound as if I am a spirit. I was afraid, too. We must do all it takes to make it tonight; remember, it is the last day. This is all I've come to tell you. I will be on my way."

"Obim, why is your friend leaving so soon? Aha, that reminds me—did you go out early today? Last night, you were not lying beside me when I woke up from sleep, though I fell asleep immediately."

"Nneoma, I went to ease myself, but it took longer than it should. Also, I heard the goats bleating, so I attended to them. Is that a problem?" He took a romantic look at her and said, "Just tell me that you are missing me."

"It's okay, but next time, let me know so I can go with you. I don't want you to get hurt," she said.

"Obim, remember that you promised to give my brother some of your goats. I think they are overcrowded, which is beginning to affect their growth."

"Yes, I will give him all the pregnant ones when he comes. All I need from him is just one nanny goat each time they deliver."

"Obim, I believe you now that I am referring to Ndudiri."

"I can never give my goat to that brother of yours—what's his name again? Ndudiri? After what he did to my farm? Never!"

"Obim, please, I am sorry. I thought that you had forgiven him. I want you to give him a second chance."

"Second chance, my foot!" said Obiagu.

-Finally, at the Grave-

They mentally shut their ears and minds to the eerie sounds permeating the blackness of the night. The forest was home to mystical creatures that could easily lure one into their lair if one fell victim to their calls.

"Ahhhh!" Obiagu jumped and started swinging his spade around hysterically.

"What... What did you see, Obiagu?" Okoye said, involuntarily thrusting his shovel in different directions and pointing the lantern toward Obiagu to illuminate the threat.

"See? Did you not hear that sound?"

"What sound?"

"Shhh! Listen!"

Okoye listened anxiously, then his countenance changed, and he gazed at Obiagu with unfiltered disappointment.

"Obiagu, for Amadioha's sake, it's just a cricket. Let's keep moving."

"Oh," Obiagu muttered bashfully.

Okoye did not seem satisfied. He continued, "Obiagu, wrestler of men, bone cruncher, number one grappler, defeater of warriors—yet it's just a cricket that made you flinch like an anxious chicken trying to save its head from the knife on Ngba festival!"

"Says the same man who was almost beaten to a pulp at Mazi Nwakali's naming ceremony. If I had not come to your defence that day, he would have punched your eyes back into their sockets," Obiagu retorted.

"Yes, and I am glad you came through for me. But what about that one time when you were drunk to stupor, and a masquerade appeared right in front of your face? Your reaction was priceless! So much fea—"

"Errr," Obiagu cut him off. "Okoye, you talk too much. Point your lantern over here... Good. We are here. This is the marker."

Obiagu gestured at a long stick embellished with a red piece of fabric. They placed the lantern and bags to the side and started to dig.

Thirty minutes later, they were still digging, the warm glow from the lantern making their sweat-laden bodies glisten.

"Finally!" Obiagu exclaimed in delight when his shovel hit something.

Okoye retorted by flinging away his shovel with abandon, panting profusely. Obiagu noticed, dipped his hand in Okoye's bag, collected a skin of water, and threw it to Okoye, who muttered some words of gratitude between pants and started gulping down the water.

"Don't die, oh," Obiagu said sarcastically while collecting his own skin of water.

Okoye ignored him, pouring the remaining water on his head and letting it drip down his body. The physical activity had taken quite a toll on him.

"Show me some light."

Okoye did as instructed.

Obiagu used his palms to smooth out the sand covering what was left of his grandmother: her skull, with dilapidated fragments of spinal bones attached to it. He turned toward Okoye, and their mouths stretched into wide grins. He took the skull, extracted the set of teeth with a unique jagged-edged knife, and put it in the bag. Then he buried the skull back, and they began to make their way out of the grave.

Little did they know that Obiagu's grandmother had been buried with a gorilla, as it was their tradition to give a befitting burial rite to the oldest among their age grade.

When they got out, they started to walk away quickly, petrified that there might be an instant repercussion.

"My renowned wrestler, why are you walking so fast?" Okoye said sarcastically.

Obiagu rolled his eyes at Okoye. "What about you?"

They both heard a sound, screamed like nine-year-olds, and took to their heels.

UDENNE'S DEMISE

Before dawn, they were at the shrine. Wonders happened when the full dental set of his dead grandmother was presented before the shrine. Unknown to Udenne (the Chief Priest), the gods hid from him the fact that any part of a gorilla brought to the shrine was a taboo. This meant that the Chief Priest and anyone who brought such an animal would surely face doom.

Immediately after he started the incantations, thunder boomed in ear-shattering frequencies. Lightning flashed in streaks of blue, embellishing the fast-expanding stormy clouds.

Udenne looked up at the sky, puzzled, but resumed his incantations. Thunder struck yet again, even more powerfully, and Udenne quit incanting. Okoye and Obiagu exchanged glances nervously. Udenne instinctively looked into the mirror, but anxiety was written all over his face. Another thunderstrike followed, and a face carved out of stormy clouds suddenly appeared in the mirror, with resounding thunder accompanying its appearance. In its eyes, streaks of blue and red lightning collided against each other. Okoye and Obiagu screamed and immediately snuggled toward each other.

"Udenne, okara nmo, okara nmadu, you have come in contact with that which is higher and stronger than you today."

The spiritual man's face expressed a blend of heart-wrenching fear and puzzlement.

"There are many things the master hides from his servants, lest they take advantage of him, and this is one of them. Today, your blood is required. You know what that means. Remember the promise I made to you when you misbehaved the last time. Goodbye!"

On the cloudy deity's last word, thunder struck, killing Udenne, Okoye, Obiagu, and even Nmirioma, who was peeling kernels at home.

Her mother, who had gone to the market, returned to find a mob barricading the front of her home, lamenting. She barged into the crowd to find out what was happening, only to see Nmirioma's body on the floor, eerily pale and lifeless. Adaobi screamed in excruciating grief, then tore her wrapper apart, saying:

"The gods have killed me today; they have put an end to the source of my happiness. What will I do without my Nmirioma?"

As she shredded her wrapper, two women instinctively ran toward her and draped a wrapper over her to protect her nakedness. They held her and tried to console her. She kept gazing into nothingness, tears streaming down her face. Slowly, she started sinking toward the ground until she was kneeling, then continued,

"The apple of my eye, she brought so much joy to me. How can the gods take my only source of bliss away?" She looked up at the sky. "What did I do to deserve this? I have wronged no one. I have always moved with good intentions, given to the needy, and always offered the first yield of each harvest to you. So tell me, what did I do to deserve this? Why did you not just take me too, so I do not have to live like this?"

"You are not dying now, Nne," a lady with a tear-stricken face said reassuringly to Adaobi while rubbing her back consolingly.

"No! It's best I die so the gods will finally be happy."

"Don't say such! You are not going anywhere. You still have your husband and us."

On hearing the word 'husband,' Adaobi jumped.

"Where is my husband?" she demanded, stretching out her hands and looking around hysterically. "Obim, please come and see what is happening..."

"Don't cry, Nne. Some youths have already gone looking for your—"

Before the woman could finish her statement, some youngsters were seen carrying the lifeless body of her beloved husband, Obiagu. The mob exclaimed in terror and grief, but no one lamented more than Adaobi. She rushed toward the body as soon as it reached the ground, embraced it, and wailed:

"OBIAGUEHHHHHHHHH!!!!!!!!!!CHINEKE MOOOOOOOOO! The gods are so wicked. They have gorged my heart out and destroyed my soul. How will I tell the story? What will I say to my people? Ohhhhh, that my husband and my daughter died on the same day? What is the cause of this sudden death? I'm going to kill myself today. What kind of fate is this? Did my daughter and my husband enter into some kind of oath that I knew nothing about? Ewoh! Chimu egbo muooo! It is best I take my life. There is nothing else to live for; the best is to join them."

She took off toward the back where her kitchen was situated to get a knife to end it, but the crowd held her back.

The news of the deaths of her husband, daughter, her husband's friend, and the spiritualist spread throughout the town. What an atrocious tragedy!

An emergency meeting was scheduled, and the elders of the land came together to consult their oracle to ascertain the reason for the deaths. They were dumbfounded when they uncovered the mystery behind it: the fact that an item that was abominable to the deity Udenne revered— the gorilla's teeth—had been presented before it, filling the deity with unbridled rage and prompting it to snuff out the lives of everyone involved.

Not long after this calamity, and totally unrelated to it, Mazi Nwosu, the old Chief Priest, gave up the ghost, and the task of officiating as the new Chief Priest now fell on Ikenna. According to the law of the land, the wife of any man killed by the gods becomes an inheritance to the Chief Priest. Whose wife would Adaobi become?

"My fellow elders, we have to see Ikenna personally and remind him of his initiation. Things are getting out of hand," cried out Mazi Okoronta, the palm wine tapper. "I suggest we fix the initiation on Orie market day, and there will be enough palm wine for both man and beast."

"Mechie onu gi! Shut up! Who is talking about palm wine? Ana ekwu na oku na agba n'ulo inachu oke," Mazi Odenigbo, a grey-haired dark man clad in a native overall, said contemptuously.

Mazi Okoronta looked at him, then around with a puzzled expression, and started indignantly, "What have I done? Is this not an open case where suggestions are needed?"

"Your head must have been blocked by that overnight palm wine of yours. That must be why you think like a fish."

"Nna lekwanu onye a o! What is upsetting you this morning? It's no one's fault that your wife gave you half-baked lovemaking last night. Stop transferring aggression."

"I see you lack respect!" Mazi Odenigbo lunged forward, wielding his walking stick as a weapon, but a fellow elder intercepted him. He continued, "No! Let me break his palm wine-filled head so it flows out, and maybe he begins to reason well."

"Silence in this place!" The oldest of them all, Mazi Ajumgbe, reprimanded. "We have an issue at hand, and both of you are busy pouring insults on each other."

"We apologize for the nuisance we caused. I've thought about it myself. It's best we go to his father's house right now! Delay may cause more harm," said Ichie Ndoni.

"Yes, you are in order," the majority of them chorused.

-Meeting at Ikenna's House-

"My elders, I greet you. You are highly welcome; here is kola nut for you." Ikenna took the tray of kola nuts from Ugochi and humbly placed it on a stool.

"Thank you, Ikenna. This is a sign of acceptance." The procedures were observed, and the kola nut was shared amicably.

Mazi Ajumgbe cleared his throat and started, "I'm sure you know why we are here. The time has come for you to take up the responsibility of the mantle that has fallen on you. The land has been polluted, and we need a Chief Priest to organize the cleansing process. Besides, the late Chief Priest cannot be buried without a Chief Priest officiating his burial rite. By our tradition, the initiation commences eight days after the death of the Chief Priest. Ikenna, from now henceforth, we consider you sacred. You must not touch anything regarded as taboo or sit together with a woman who has not reached menopause, lest she defile you. My elders, am I right?"

"Yes, you've spoken well," the elders chorused.

All the while, Ikenna listened with rapt attention, his eyes fixated on the leftover kola nut on the tray. He made sure the elder was done with his speech before he stood and, without a stutter, said, "My elders, thank you for the opportunity to stand and speak before you. As you all know, I'm still mourning the death of my father, and to be honest, I'm not interested in taking up the mantle."

The elders exclaimed simultaneously, "EHWOOOOOO. ARU EME! An abomination has taken place."

"Can you explain to us why you don't want to take up the mantle again?" Mazi Ajumgbe asked, visibly disturbed.

"Thank you once again. How do you expect me to get married to a woman old enough to be my mother? You didn't even seek my opinion. I have a woman I want to marry, and I've already proposed to her. My teacher back in my school days always told me that I'm a promising child, and my friends tell me the same too. With that in mind, I've decided to acquire higher education. Finally, my elders, I've given my life to Christ. The priest who comes to the town hall teaches us things contrary to what I hear the custodians of the oracle do. I heard him say clearly that this God is a merciful God, and I'm in love with this God—that's why I gave my life to Him. If only my father and his friend had sought help from the Almighty God, He would have given them children, and they wouldn't have died the way they did. My parents made their mistakes in the past, and I'm not ready to make the same mistake."

"God forbid! Ikenna, we don't understand all the things you've been saying. Are you trying to say that our gods are not merciful? Or that they have not been giving children to the barren? Just for your information, there is no god higher than the gods of our fathers. They protect us, give us rain, and bless us with bountiful harvests each year. As you can see, it's the yield from the previous harvest that we use to marry new wives, just as I married another woman two weeks ago—making my wives three. That means I am blessed. I will have more children to help work on the farm. Ikenna, whether you accept it or not, you must be the next Chief Priest. It is you that the oracle has chosen. Your initiation will take place as we have stipulated. Ndi Ichie, let's go and fine-tune everything," Ichie Ndini said.

Chapter 6 | Ikenna Missing

Early in the morning, the villagers, especially older women and young men were seen in different groups clearing the bushy pathways, sweeping their community, and burning debris in preparation for Ikenna's initiation and his marriage ceremony. Here came Odochi, Ikenna's cousin, who told them about Ikenna's disappearance for the past two days.

"My god! I was getting ready to go and see him and tell him some of our secrets before his initiation," said Ichie Ndoni. "Odochi, my daughter, are you sure of what you are saying?"

"Yes, Ichie, you can come and see things for yourself. It is my mother who sent me."

"If I may ask, where is your father?" Ichie Okafor asked.

"He has been in pain at home for the past four days," Odochi replied.

"What! Is he sick? Why hasn't he sent for any of us?"

"I don't know. I think he wants to be left alone. Please come and help him; I don't want him to die," said Odochi, tears glimmering in her eyes.

"For the last time, what is his reason for hiding his sickness from us?" Ichie Okafor asked.

"Enough! Ichie Okafor, you ask too many questions. Let's do the needful—first things first. We must contact Ikechi, the town crier, so that he can announce his search," said Ichie Ndoni.

The news of Ikenna's disappearance came as a surprise to his people. While they were busy searching for his whereabouts, Ikenna was already heading toward Umukam, where he had seen Reverend John on one of their school outings. Upon his arrival, the priest prepared for a journey—a school outing with the pupils from the remote learning quarters. After narrating his story to the priest, the latter felt sorry for him and ordered some food for him.

"By the way, what is your name?" the priest asked collectedly, his lips creased into a sincere smile.

"My name is Ikenna Maduabuchi Ikenna," Ikenna said, his eyelashes interweaving beautifully when he blinked.

"I admire your courage. You are going to grow into a brave man. I know that by now, your people must be looking for you. Time will not permit me to take you back home today. All the same, you are in good hands. Stay here until I come back from my journey."

"Sir, I can't stay here without you. Please take me with you," Ikenna said, running to the priest and holding him tightly. The reverend was now in a sober mood. He also wrapped his hands around Ikenna, looked up and down, and shook his head in dismay. Then he said to Ikenna, "My dear Ikenna, going with you is not a problem. It's just that I will be away for some months. Missionary work is not an easy task. You are still a child, and I am not sure you will be able to withstand some of the challenges we face out there."

Ikenna wore a sad frown, and the reverend highlighted why he could not tag along. But he was sensible enough to know that the reverend cared about his well-being, so he obediently obliged. The thoughts of the rites and rituals awaiting him back in his village petrified him.

"Bu...but I can stay here with the seminarians?" Ikenna asked in a mellow tone, but you could spot the desperation in his eyes.

"Of course you can, Ikenna. There's a lot you will learn here. A whole lot," the reverend replied in the gentlest tone ever, rubbing Ikenna's head affectionately. Ikenna grinned.

So, he stayed with some of the seminarians. Day after day, he began to settle in.

Back in the village, there was buzzing tension everywhere as Ikenna was nowhere to be found.

"By the way, Ichie Okafor, we cannot lose two things at the same time. There is no wisdom in that. Let us go and see Mazi Metu, who has been sick for some days now," said Ichie Ndoni among the village councilmen, who were sprawled underneath a mango tree, their cups of palm wine thoroughly unattended. How gloomy could the atmosphere be that they wouldn't indulge in their regular merry drink?

As if being puppeteered, they all stood and began to walk in the direction leading to Mazi Metu's home.

"If you say so. I don't want another insult; otherwise, I would have asked another question," Ichie Okafor said indignantly.

"You have started again. Save it until we get there."

"Ichie Ndoni, people like you don't learn things fast," Ichie Okafor countered speedily, not letting the embers totally die out. It was as if he had prepared for trouble. "My father of blessed memory told us when he was alive that people who don't ask questions when they should make lots of mistakes."

Ichie Ndoni stopped walking abruptly and turned squarely toward Okafor, giving him unbreakable attention. "Okafor, my own father told me that people who ask too many questions get themselves into trouble."

"The gods forbid! Your father was not well taught!" Ichie Okafor exclaimed.

The men began to mutter.

"Shut your mouth, Okafor!" escaped from an unidentified male among the group of councilmen, who were now moving like an angry mob.

"Are you trying to insult my father?" Ichie Ndoni asked, gesticulating with his right palm on his chest, his eyes burning with rage.

"Not at all! I am just trying to defend what my father told me!" Ichie Okafor said in a less hostile tone. He knew Ndoni could turn him upside down and plant his head underneath the surface of the dirt if he probed further.

"There's no need to quarrel. That's the house," Ichie Ndoni said, pointing toward a mud house with a thatched roof, hardly different from every other home in the village. It would take them less than 30 seconds to get there. "When we get there, you can ask all your questions, but I can assure you that you must come back home with a broken head," Ichie Ndoni retorted.

Ichie Okafor yelped anxiously upon hearing that and then struggled to compose himself. Then he started defiantly, "See me o, why are you taking it personally? Did you not insult me, too?" Then he gestured at everyone. "Thank goodness there are witnesses here because it would not be funny."

"Okafor, please just shut up. Always rambling like a convulsing chicken. Have you not had your fill already?" someone said.

"Leave him. Now he is cowering away from a fight his big mouth started," another echoed.

"May pythons swallow you both alive, possessed monkeys!" Ichie Okafor fired back at his enemies.

As they passed the lengthy shrubs preventing optimum vision, they were bamboozled to see a crowd at the entrance.

"That reminds me of the incident at the shrine," Okafor started. He was inches ahead of them, deliberately staying out of Ichie Ndoni's way to avoid being smothered into unconsciousness by his beastly arms. "Let me ask this woman. I saw her just come out of Metu's house."

When she got close, he called, "Oriaku, please don't be offended. Can I ask you a question?"

The black lady, clad in a palm-leaf-patterned brown wrapper, ignored him, a frown plastered on her face.

"Hello? I'm asking..." Okafor said, hurrying after her, looking over his shoulder to see who was chuckling at him. The lady did not break her pace.

"Don't ask me. I am not ready to answer any questions. Please go away; I don't want people to say again that I am cheating on my husband."

Okafor stood, totally puzzled. He did not know what to make of the woman's reply.

"Who are you? Who is this woman?" he inquired contemptuously, visibly annoyed.

"Ichie Okafor, are you the only person who is blind in this village? Is this not the wife of Kamma, who was caught in adultery and was penalized?"

"Oh. She is looking emaciated; that is why I can no longer recognize her."

"Look at a man coming; he may have answers to your endless questions," said Mazi Ndoni sarcastically. Ichie Okafor shot a deathly look at him and then turned toward the old, fair-complexioned man approaching them.

Ichie Okafor continued in his curiosity, "Nnanyi, please wait. Let me ask you something. There's been a rumour flying around about Metu's demise. Is this true?"

"Em, well... everything is in the gods' hands. I can see that you are heading toward his house. When you get there, you will see things for yourself. Ka emesia."

"But you are just coming from there. It would not hurt if you told—" While Ichie Okafor rambled away, the rest of the elders were already walking through Metu's door.

"Hey! You guys should slow down now!" Ichie Okafor exclaimed while hurrying toward them. "This must be a very serious matter. No one is ready to tell us the true position of things."

Before one could say 'Jack,' Mazi Ndoni was already inside the house. He was completely horror-stricken by what he saw. Okafor stepped in, muttering incomprehensible words, but as soon as 'it' entered his vision, his face began to turn pale, and his tongue was firmly glued to his mouth. They stayed for some minutes, gazing wide-eyed, trying to process what they saw, and then left without saying anything.

Odochi ran after them.

"My elders, why do you leave? I thought you had come to help him. Please come back!"

"Odochi, my daughter, it's obvious that your father's ailment is strange. Can't you see the way he is lying lifeless? In fact, if you don't look well, you would think that he is dead. This is the kind of situation where my people say that such a person is in between the land of the living and the land of the dead. This is not the case when prescribing some herbs; otherwise, I would have done so. But apparently, I can do nothing. There is a need to consult the oracle. Don't worry, we will be back soon," said Ichie Ndoni.

"Ichie Ndoni, you seem to forget so fast. Which oracle are you going to consult? Can't you remember that Nwaosu is dead and Ikenna is yet to be found? From the look of things, it seems that he has defecated in a deity's lair in the evil forest. Or what do you think?"

"Please, Mazi Okafor, leave me out of this. Ikenna is our major problem. Ikenna, of course, must be found. I just hope we meet him at home so that the initiation can commence."

Chapter 7 | Reverend John Transforms Village Life

Though it was a stressful journey, Rev. John arrived safely at Umodo Village, looking pale and worn out. The people were already expecting him, so it wasn't a problem to accord him a heartwarming welcome. Some women had already prepared akpu with ofe akwu in anticipation of his visit. Most of the villagers were fish farmers. They had rivers running through their land. These rivers were actually a sight to behold—the water was as clear as crystal, and everyone drew from them. No matter how little one took, it quenched their thirst. It was a wonder of nature because situated at the belly of the river, it was a mighty stone that caused the waters to circumvent to the other side in a breathtaking manner. That was the climax of the beauty of this river—so unique, I must say.

At the riverbank, little children could be seen frolicking, singing, and chanting their local songs while their mothers fetched water. On the other hand, some villagers gathered for ritual purposes.

Spreading the good news of our Lord Jesus wasn't a problem for Reverend John because many people were already tired of the way things were. The incessant killing of twins as well as virgins was one of the few customary rites that the villagers considered outdated. The fact that their deities always demanded items that required almost inhumane strength and wisdom to extract was something they could not wrap their heads around. Reverend John did not stop at just preaching the Gospel; he also introduced new packages and innovations that attracted many people, especially women and youths. Every Saturday after evangelism, some of the youths gathered at the Reverend's premises to learn skills such as soap and pomade making, given the abundance of palm kernels in the village. After several weeks, some of the villagers, who were naturally dexterous, had grasped the skills well and had become quite proficient. They, in turn, helped the Reverend train others. In return, these people were grateful to Reverend John and equally thanked their "Chi" for bringing him their way, as their means of livelihood had greatly improved.

It had been four months since Reverend John arrived in the village. He was really worried, not knowing what was happening back home. He decided to write two letters—one to Ikenna and the other to the mission. He did not forget to pen down some of the progress he had made in Umodo while preaching the gospel. He also reminded them not to neglect the assembly of the brethren and to always uphold him in prayers. In the letter he sent to Ikenna, he instructed him to get ready to accompany him on his next visit.

Ikenna glimmered with excitement upon reading that he would join the Reverend on his next visit but was a bit disconcerted, knowing it would be in the next two months. Two months felt terrifically long! Even though the seminarians treated him nicely, he felt his sanity peeling away at the thought of being unfulfilled, unable to work side by side with the Reverend.

A mischievous thought slipped into his mind, and he grinned. He scanned upward, fixed his eyes on the far-right corner of the letter where the Reverend had written his address, and thought, *I am tired of staying here. Now that I have his address, I must pay him a surprise visit. It is obvious that I cannot spend the remaining two months without seeing him. I must leave first thing tomorrow morning—but not without my breakfast.*

Ikenna, who did not know the way to Umodo, deliberately avoided asking anyone for directions because he did not want them to suspect his movement. As a result, he lost his way and walked in circles. Evening came, and the only place he could rest his head was the village square. Little did he know that he had entered the land of Umuabali, a village that had just lost its king and required the heads of three strangers to give him a befitting burial.

In this village, being chosen for the headhunt was considered a noble task. Those who knew about this custom imposed an early curfew on their households for fear of losing their lives. Poor Ikenna, weak and exhausted from the unnecessarily long journey, slumbered in a little hut he had spotted in the square.

Meanwhile, three men had set out hunting for strangers' heads. They searched through deserted roads and narrow paths but found nothing. Suddenly, they walked through the market square, and one of them decided to peep into the hut. There, he saw a boy lying like a log of wood, his mouth gaping open, with a drool on the right corner of his lips. Discreetly, he nudged the others to come and see, a sly smile patched on his weathered face. When they saw Ikenna, they put their heads together to decide what to do.

They chose not to wake him up immediately. However, as they argued in hushed tones, their rambling roused him from sleep. He woke up with a start and shouted for help. One of them gestured at him to keep quiet.

"Who are you, and what are you doing here at this time of the day?" one of them demanded.

Ikenna, stammering, explained that he had embarked on a journey to see someone but had lost his way. The men looked at each other before one of them spoke again.

"You need not be afraid," he said. "Follow us, and we will show you the right way. You will be safe because we are the village guards."

Okwe, one of the guards, said among the rest of them, out of Ikenna's hearing, "Today seems to be a lucky day for us. I suggest that we keep him until the search is over. As we all know, one head has not been provided. Who knows? A handsome reward might be offered to anyone who can provide the remaining head. He will be useful since he is not from this community."

"Not bad at all! But let's bind him and keep him in our hut on the grounds that he is an infiltrator from another village who has come to gather intel. This way, he would think there is a tangible reason for keeping him, and he would never know the real deal."

They nodded approvingly at the idea and bound him.

"I thought you said you would help me! Why are you binding my arms?"

"Well, we cannot just buy the story you told us. For all we know, you could be a spy sent to find a weakness in our community. Soon, you may give a signal, and a legion of warriors could behead every single man and take our women and harvest."

"But... I am innocent! I tell you no lies."

"Quiet! Okwe, make it tighter. That thing seems easy to wiggle out of."

Two days passed, and nothing had been done. Ikenna was neither freed, punished, nor killed, and this made him even more anxious about his fate. He pondered over how the seminarians had found out that he was missing and how they might have searched every nook and cranny for his whereabouts. It was possible that they had written to the Reverend, and he imagined the poor man being worried sick, kneeling by his bed and praying fervently for him. He felt foolish for embarking on the journey.

While he nursed the roasted yam dipped in palm oil, the guards sat a few inches from him, rambling noisily about the voluptuous women they had met on their way to the stream, comparing which woman had the bigger hips. Unbridled anxiety made his stomach curl and the meal bitter. He grew increasingly uncomfortable and eventually confronted them. They promised to come up with a decision about what to do with him soon.

That evening, Ikenna overheard them discussing him. He was shocked when he heard them fighting over how the money would be shared after providing his head since the people originally delegated to do so had failed.

In the middle of the night, he ran away. He ran so fast that he stumbled into an old woman carrying a lantern in a basket. The woman asked him where he was running to at that hour of the night. His heart pounded in fear.

"I am going to Umodo. I lost my way."

"In that case, follow this path to your left and don't look back until you reach the next junction. Take a right, go straight, and it will lead you to a market. Stay there till dawn. Ask anyone about Reverend John, and you will be taken to him."

"Did I hear you say, Reverend John? How did you know that he is the one I am looking for? By the way, what are you doing here? Did you lose your way too?"

"You wouldn't understand, my son. I stay around this area every night to protect those who need protection and to fight the wicked ones."

"You must be a kind person. Don't you think your children will be looking for you at this time of the night?"

"Ha! Who are you, little boy? You must be brave to look me in the eyes and ask such a question. Leave now! Say no more before you lose your protection," the old woman said.

Ikenna took in her features again, just to be sure: a wrinkled face, a hunched back, and a hand that shakily held the lantern.

How could she possibly kill a mosquito when she couldn't even grip something as light as a lantern? Ikenna wondered.

Meanwhile, Jeku, who had gone to use the bathroom, decided to check on Ikenna. On arriving, he noticed Ikenna wasn't in the house—he had escaped! Okwe and Jeku decided to run after him while Uche refused to tag along.

Jeku said to Okwe as they scampered around the hut, checking for fresh footprints and trying to guess which pathway Ikenna had taken, "Don't be discouraged by Uche's nonchalant attitude. By the time we get the boy, we will share the money amongst ourselves."

Uche, who stood indifferently by a corner, mindlessly sheathing and unsheathing his knife, replied, "You are free to share the money with Okwe because I have no interest in it and will not partake in blood money. I know money is one of my major challenges, but I will not accept any ill-gotten wealth."

They ignored him and ran as fast as they could after Ikenna. On their way, they saw the same old woman and asked if she had seen a little boy running through that path. But the old woman ignored them and pretended not to have heard.

Angrily, they repeated the question, threatening to strangle her if she played dumb again. She misled them in the wrong direction. They called her a witch and turned to leave, but she called them back. As they turned to see why she was calling them, they went blind immediately. She led them into the evil forest, where they could not find their way out, and left them there to suffer and die.

Ikenna ran safely to the market square, where he finally felt secure. At last, he was relieved when he saw Reverend John warmly interacting with a woman selling vegetables, occasionally playing with the chubby baby in her arms. When the Reverend saw Ikenna, he was shocked, and they strolled away from the busy crowd. Ikenna quickly narrated his ordeal.

Reverend John was deeply moved. "My dear," he said, "all these trials you're going through show that you have a destiny to fulfil. I had a terrible dream about you a few days ago, but all thanks to God, who has delivered you. But, my dear, learn this: never run away to a place you are not familiar with. You may end up in a worse state—or worse still, you may lose your life. You have been saved by the grace of God."

Ikenna nodded frantically. He imagined those devious guards laying him on a table, slicing off his head first and then the rest of his body into chunky bits. He almost flinched at the thought and agreed that it was indeed God who had saved him.

"You must be hungry. Let's go back into the market. I need to get some greens—it's the only ingredient missing. I want to prepare the tastiest Oha soup ever!"

Ikenna smiled at the statement and tagged along.

Within a few days, Ikenna had rested and felt stronger and better. He assisted Reverend John in educating people on how to read and write. After two months, his stay in Umodo came to an end. Many gifts were presented to him by the villagers in appreciation of his love and help toward them. He was truly overwhelmed and thanked them immensely for their generosity and kindness, but he couldn't accept their gifts. Instead, he pleaded with them to sell the gifts and use the money to buy land for the church. The villagers were astonished! How could a person be so kind-hearted? In addition to their gifts, one of the villagers, Mr. Nwachukwu, who had greatly impacted Reverend John's ministry, donated his land to the church.

Two days had passed, and Okwe and Jeku were nowhere to be found. Uche was worried because they were part of his squad. Other village guards who were not on duty that night began questioning him seriously about their whereabouts. Among the guards were some who were not on good terms with Uche; they yelled at him and pushed him around, demanding the truth. However, he maintained his narrative, but they found it hard to believe. One of the guards, Onyeike, accused him of foul play and promised to expose him soon.

The families of the missing men reported the issue to the village heads, and Uche was interrogated once again. He narrated the entire story to them. The village heads, being elderly and wise, carefully considered the matter and said to Uche, "We are not saying that your hands are clean, but we will be back soon. In the meantime, as a village guard, do you know of any hidden paths around your house?"

"Yes, behind my house, past that old and deserted hut... Oh, I can't remember the name of the man who lived there, although he is late now. Oh! His name was Onyedibia."

"Onyedibia? Ha. Growing up, we heard a lot of strange stories about that area. Anyway, that will be all for now," Ojukwu said. As they walked back, they discussed the way forward.

Three days later, four women returning from one of their farthest farms came back and reported to their husbands about a stench they had perceived and how vultures were gathering in that area. Mma's husband asked them, "What are you insinuating? This is not the first time you women have perceived a foul smell."

Mma, his wife, responded, "To be frank, Nnanyi Utaba, the odor is like that of a rotting corpse."

"Meshie gi onnu ebehu ino! How do you tell the difference in a stench? To me, a stench is a stench. Period."

"Nnanyi, you know that during the Biafran war, there were many dead bodies around us. I could easily recognize the smell of a decomposing body."

"This is serious! Women, don't worry. Please go home and freshen up; we will look into it."

The following day, the husbands of these women reported the matter to the village heads, who immediately summoned the village guards. The location was described to them, and they were sent to investigate and report back to the village. When they arrived, they were horrified to find that the corpses were indeed those of the two missing guards. Their bodies were swollen and had turned dark.

"What could have happened to them?" Uche asked in amazement.

Chapter 8 | Erinma Reveals the Secret

Everyone at the mission church in Umukam was happy to have Reverend John and Ikenna back in their midst. One week later, the Reverend reminded Ikenna of the need to go with him to his village.

"By the way, Ikenna, who was that Erinma girl, and what was she doing in Umodo?"

"Oh, Erinma? We were classmates, and Umodo is her maternal home."

"Ok, that is fine, but you just have to be careful because I saw the way you were staring at her," said Reverend John.

"Oh," Ikenna said, chuckling shyly.

Back in Aguata, strange things were happening, and the search for Ikenna continued with no results. This time, the elders agreed to work with another priest since theirs was dead and the presumed successor had fled the land. They decided to visit the renowned Ogwueke shrine of Umunta. They would have to journey through demon-lurking hills and murky swamps.

"Okafor, I learned that it takes four days to get to Umunta, but whatever it takes, we must get there because we can't continue to fold our arms and watch our cattle and our children die from strange diseases. If you and I can't go because of age, we can appoint younger people to go," said Mazi Ndoni, the worried creases on his face cascading with the wrinkles on his forehead.

Three days later, Mazi Ukaegbu and Mazi Ntiga embarked on the journey to Umunta village. The first day was not rough.

They trudged through the bank of a swamp, discussing intensely.

"Mazi Ntiga, since we've been walking and talking, one thing has been bothering me. Why do our elders always send you and me on errands like this? Are they bigger and better than us? I'm beginning to suspect foul play," said Ukaegbu.

"Don't let it bother you. I have discovered over the years that some people are used as scapegoats in some communities. But wait! Did you remember this because you are hungry?" Ntiga asked.

"Yes, Ntiga. I am both hungry and angry. What we have left is very little." Ukaegbu shook his animal skin bag pitifully, draped over his shoulder.

"Oh! You should have said so! I have a rich in-law in this village; my sister is married to him. We may pass the night in their home," Ukaegbu said.

"If you say so, I don't have any other choice," Ukaegbu retorted, pausing before following the new direction Ntiga led.

After roughly twenty-five minutes of sweat-laden rambling, they arrived at their destination and were bathed in immeasurable hospitality.

"Mazi Ntiga, look at the rousing welcome your in-law gave us. Poverty is not good at all. I have said it countless times—my only daughter must be married to a very rich and liberal man."

"Ya gazie," Ntiga echoed. "My joy is that we slept well last night," he added.

Finally, upon reaching the shrine at Umunta, the chief priest told them it would cost them a great fortune to consult the oracle. They looked at each other and then turned back to him.

The Chief Priest began the incantations and told them to return in a month's time as his chi (god) wasn't ready to give them answers. They were not happy hearing the news but departed anyway. It took them another four days to arrive home. The people at home were waiting eagerly to hear from them. Upon telling the villagers what the Chief Priest had said, they were disappointed, and their spirits sank.

Unknown to Ikenna, Erinma had excitedly told her family the other day that she had seen him. Upon hearing this news, her father did not hesitate to relay the message to the council of elders. The elders forced Erinma to take them to the place where she had seen Ikenna. Upon their arrival, he was not there. Out of fear of wasting the elders' time, Erinma's father scolded her, asking if she wanted to disgrace him before the council of elders.

"Erinma, I thought you said you saw him here?"

"Yes, Papa, I saw him here, and I remember telling you that he may not be here again before we embarked on this journey. But you people wouldn't listen to me."

She was hushed by one of the elders.

"Erinma, this is no longer a family matter, and from your statement, we know you know his whereabouts. So take us to him before worse things happen," Ichie Okafor said sternly.

Erinma's father responded to Ichie Okafor abruptly, "What worse things? What wrong has my daughter done by bringing us here?"

Ichie Okafor attacked without hesitation. "Mazi, just pay attention to what you just said. How sure are we that you and your daughter have not connived and hidden him for your selfish interest?"

"Watch your tongue, Okafor," Erinma's father warned, then turned to his daughter. "Erinma, where else do you think we could find him?"

"All she told me was that he would go to Umukam."

"Ok. Where exactly in Umukam?"

"Father, I don't know."

"How on earth are we supposed to search for a young man with so little information in an unknown land?" a chief complained.

"You see why I think they've hidden him for selfish gains?" Okafor added, raising his brow cockily. "Umukam is quite a distance from here. The roads are bad, too, and I learned that there's an evil forest in that village. I, Ichie Okafor, do not want to die like a chicken. I should die honourably in my house. The gods forbid that I, Ichie Okafor, die a careless death. After all, my only son is dead." He muttered a few words under his breath and left.

The others continued with the journey. Though they were afraid, duty called for the task. They searched for him on high and low mountains and later found him wrapped around Reverend John like a baby who had just been weaned from his mother's breast.

"Ikenna is that you, stubborn child!" said Isiguzo. "You can run fast, but you cannot hide. Look at the pain and trouble you've brought to your people, and here you are, feeling so relaxed!"

Mazi Isiguzo and others accused the Reverend of kidnapping Ikenna and insisted that Ikenna must come along with them immediately. Ikenna refused to go with them and shouted, beckoning the Reverend for help, but the Reverend had little or nothing he could do.

They journeyed back home. The villagers, upon seeing them return with Ikenna, were very happy, believing that an end had come to their calamities, not knowing what Ikenna had in mind.

"Where is Ichie Okafor?" asked Ichie Ndoni. "Tell him that we are back with good news— Ikenna is here with us."

"Which Okafor are you talking about?"

"Hear him! What kind of question is that? How many Okafors do we have in this village? Or do you want me to remind you of how his elder brother, Okafor, the bald-headed man with a potbelly, died after stealing a goat from Agbala's shrine?" Mazi Ndoni responded.

"Ichie Ndoni, calm down. It has not come to that. I think he is just confused. But Echidime, what sort of question is that?" Isiguzo asked.

"Mazi Isiguzo, please see me, oh! I was just trying to tell him that the Okafor in question is dead. I guess he was angry on arrival."

"Wait, wait, and wait! What are you talking about? Do you mean that Ichie Okafor is dead? When did this happen?"

"He died two days after he returned from Umodo and told us that he couldn't continue with you people."

"You don't mean it! What was the cause of his death? Did he die honourably like the king of the jungle?"

"In fact, he died a shameful death. He slipped on a little child's faeces, and that was all."

"What a shame. Maybe if he had stayed back with us, he wouldn't be dead by now. From the way he was behaving the last time, I'm forced to believe that some ancestral spirits were running after him, and eventually, they've sent him to the great beyond."

"What a pity! Just from the way he died, he can't be an ancestor because he did not die a good death," another lamented.

"Ichie Ndoni, you are passing judgment already. Are you one of the ancestors? Wait a minute."

"Wait, what?! You had better stop so we could do the needful."

"My elders, you are welcome," Adanma interrupted with her greeting.

"Ehee, Adanma, so you are even around, and I am here wasting my saliva talking to that thing? Anyway, go to the house of our town crier and tell him to sound the gong around the village, informing the people that Ikenna is here with us. Echidime, you can assist him."

"Wait a minute, Ichie Ndoni. It would be good if we could hear from Ikenna. It has been a while since he ran away from home, and perhaps he may have changed his mind," Mazi Isiguzo remarked.

"Mazi Isiguzo, sometimes I wonder if you are a bona fide son of this land. Can't you understand that Ikenna does not have a mind of his own? He was chosen by the gods, so he cannot run away from it. If he does, he will not live to tell the story. The very moment the villagers gather, his initiation will commence. There are no two ways about it."

Quite a number of people came out, though some were not at home as they might be preoccupied with farming or business. The town crier addressed the people, as was their custom.

"People of Aguata, you are welcome. I can see the sign of relief on your faces. Even the weather is happy. Look at how the leaves are dancing with the wind—this emphasizes the fact that the gods will soon be appeased because our son Ikenna is here with us." He abruptly turned to Ikenna.

"Could you please tell the people the reason you ran away?"

Ikenna hesitantly took two steps forward, glanced at the roaring number of faces in front of him, heaved, and began,

“My people, you are all welcome. I ran away because I was no longer interested in serving your gods. It was a decision made by your gods and not by me.”

Hisses and sneers escaped the crowd on hearing his words. Nevertheless, he continued.

“I have decided to serve the only true and living God, and—”

“May the gods fire your mouth!” Isiguzo retorted with rage. “Are you saying that the gods your father introduced you to are dead? We know that this Reverend has brainwashed you.”

“You accuse me falsely. I don’t have power of my own; it is the work of the Holy Spirit. I want to use this opportunity to tell you about the love of Jesus Christ, the son of God. He paid for the debt of our sins by His death on the cross. If you are willing to come to Him today, He is ever ready to save you if only—”

“Mechie onu gi! Close your mouth!” Isiguzo retorted. “Look at him! Are we captives in our father’s land? What are you even insinuating, this man? In fact, we have had enough of this fairy tale. John, or whatever you call yourself, do you think that changing your name to a white man’s name makes you superior to us? You lie! You and Ikenna must face the wrath of our gods. You must be sacrificed to the idol. Where are the strong men of our land? Bind them and take them to Aguba shrine. We have heard enough of this nonsense,” Isiguzo said.

Before he could finish his sentence, four able-bodied men from the crowd pounced on them both with strong ropes.

“Yes!”

“Bind them both!”

“Their punishment is long overdue!” the villagers chanted affirmatively.

"Ikenna, have you forgotten me, Ichie Ndoni, your father's friend? What has come over you that you have failed to listen to me? I still want you to reconsider. Help yourself and help us!"

"Where are you taking me? Leave me alone! You can't do this to me!" Ikenna said while trying to resist, but he was ignored. He repeated this over and over, but it didn't make any difference until they finally arrived at Aguba shrine.

"Put him down and tie him to that oha tree."

The villagers encircled them and kept chanting words like:

"Dismember the fake white man!"

"Cut him limb from limb and serve him to the dogs!"

Meanwhile, the Reverend Father remained calm and could be seen silently muttering words.

Isiguzo stepped forward.

"Ikenna, you have been given ten minutes to reconsider your decision."

Ikenna turned toward the Reverend, who gestured for him to remain calm. Then he went on his knees.

"My God, I did not know that it would get to this point, but my Bible tells me that when we call on You in times of trouble, You hear us. Lord, I want You to do a miracle in the life of Ikenna and me, which will be a sign before these people. In Jesus' name, I pray. Amen."

"A stubborn fly goes to the grave with the corpse. And you, Ikenna, what have you got to say? Since you have chosen to be stubborn and rebel against the will of our gods, we are going to sacrifice your blood to them. Set them ablaze!" said Isiguzo.

Chapter 9 | The Sacrifice

Just as they were about to be burned, a very loud thunderclap was heard, and the shrine of Aguba caught fire. The ropes tied around them were broken, everyone took to their heels, and those who had gone to the farm were running helter-skelter. The community was in disarray. Ikenna was amazed! The Reverend, who was mature in spiritual matters, knew that it was God's intervention. He called on the people to come back and hear the word of the Lord. No one paid attention; they had never seen such a terrible thing before.

Ikenna and the Reverend slept at the Aguba shrine. They were both tired and hungry when they woke up the following day. The Reverend was thinking about what to do next. He looked up and saw some people coming towards the shrine. Some of the people had run away the previous day and returned to see things for themselves. They were petrified when they saw Ikenna and the Reverend alive and ran off again. The Reverend stood up and called them back.

"We are not spirits but flesh and blood, just like you. What happened yesterday was a sign to show you that we serve the Almighty God. Accept Him, and you will be saved today."

There was silence everywhere. Reverend John noticed their fear. He stepped closer and repeated what he had said before. Erinma was the first to come forward, and the others followed her. Ikenna was happy to see her; he led them to Christ and gave thanks to God.

After the fellowship, Ikenna, whose stomach was rumbling, asked Erinma to get him some food, and she cheerfully went off. When she got home, she packed some fufu and fisherman's soup, which she had prepared the previous night, and was about to leave when her father intercepted her. He gave her and the package a stern look.

"Erinma, where are you taking my food?"

She was dumbfounded, knowing fully well that she had been caught. He continued,

"Erinma, is that why Ichie Okafor was reprimanding me? So you want to take my food to that OSU? I see that you want the wrath of the gods to fall upon our family. Go and call my friend Mazi Onukwufo; we must follow you to that place."

She immediately left, and in less than fifteen minutes, she returned with Mazi Onukwufo.

"Mazi Isiguzo, I was already getting ready to go there before your daughter arrived. Some of the youths told me what happened yesterday at the shrine, and they also told me what happened this morning. Are you telling me you haven't heard that your daughter was the first to accept the God of that rebellious boy called Ikenna?"

At that moment, Mazi Isiguzo's eyes were bloodshot with rage. Erinma shivered with fear.

"Erinma, tell me this is a lie."

Erinma gazed back, her entire being shuddering with intense fear. Isiguzo reached out fiercely, pulled her hair, and she screamed from the searing pain.

"You stupid girl! Is that so? No wonder! Let's go there first; I will show them what I'm made of."

He yanked her toward the direction of the Aguba shrine, and Mazi Onukwufo followed.

When they finally arrived, they saw that the entire shrine had been razed, just as everyone had described. Isiguzo glanced at the Reverend, then back at the demolished shrine, and then at the Reverend again as if asking what had happened. The Reverend wore a calm smile and did not flinch.

Ikenna emerged from behind one of the bushes, having gone to relieve himself. He stopped and joined the silent staring.

"Mazi Onukwufo, I learned that when Christianity first came to this village, it was my grandfather who stopped it. The only thing they accepted was education. In other communities, you can see churches, but not here. Some of our people who follow the white man's religion go to the neighbouring village to pray. You know how we treat them; we blame them for every evil in this village. But since this god cannot fight for himself, I am too small to fight for him. I am going to do exactly what my daughter did. I don't know about you."

"Mazi Isiguzo, you may be right, but what do you think our people will say?"

"Mazi Onukwufo, I was here yesterday. They all ran away. I see that this is a personal decision."

He turned to Erinma.

"My daughter, call the Reverend for me. I don't want to hinder the furtherance of the gospel either."

"Neither do I intend to do so. Yes, Erinma, call him for both of us."

The Reverend began, "Brethren, we are going to use this shrine as our place of worship for now. You don't have to be afraid; you have seen that we serve the Almighty God and that all power belongs to Him. Before I announce our fellowship days, we must return to Umukam to prepare and come back. Of course, our people over there will be worried about us. Before we go, please don't forget to say this prayer every day until we return: 'JESUS, YOU ARE WELCOME INTO MY LIFE. ALL POWER BELONGS TO YOU. AMEN.'"

The newfound faith of Mazi Isiguzo and his friend became the talk of the town. His kinsmen could not believe that someone like Mazi Isiguzo could be swayed so easily. They had seen him as one of the tools to destroy any intruder in their community, but now that he had joined, they wondered what to do.

"Nnanyi Isiguzo, this is the first time you've made a decision without telling me. Now that you have joined the white man's religion, what are you going to do with all those graven images you kept here? So you want to deprive me of my right? You had better come back and finish what you started. As for me, I will continue with what you introduced me to, old fool."

"Obiageli, come back here! Has it come to that? Come here, I said! Come back here! I demand an apology."

"Apology, my foot! Yesterday, five people came with five fowls for the usual sacrificial routine, and you didn't accept them. Now tell me, what are we going to eat? This is just the beginning of insults until you learn to use your head. Anu mpam."

After four days, Reverend John, Ikenna, and two seminarians, Simon and Noah, returned. They prayed and offered praises to the Lord at the Aguba shrine.

"Bia, Isiguzo, where are you going at this time of day?" Obiageli inquired, chasing after her husband.

"Obiageli, I don't know what has come over you. If you must know, I am going for a fellowship. Erinma, I hope you're ready so we can go to Onukwufo's house and then to the service from there."

"Yes, Nnanyi," Erinma replied, tying a multi-coloured scarf on her head.

"Erinma, where do you think you are going?" Have you finished pounding the pepper I told you to pound?"

"Yes, Nne."

"What about the firewood I asked you to get?"

"Nne, I will do that when I come back."

"I can see that you people are not serious. When you come back, you will eat my head."

"Obiageli, there is some firewood over there; you can make use of it," Mazi Isiguzo said matter-of-factly.

"Did I hear you call that thing firewood? Let me tell you, a lizard has urinated on them, and they will not burn well."

"I can see that you are going crazy."

"Papa Erinma, you are the one who is going crazy."

"Obiageli, if you think that you can distract me from where I am going, you are lying. Ada, let's go."

"Like father, like daughter—apparently the same. Black goat."

Isiguzo and his daughter hurried to his friend's house, and they went together for the fellowship.

-After The Fellowship-

"Erinma, why have I not seen my cousin Odochi? Is she well at all?" said Ikenna.

"So you have not heard that your uncle Metu died from a strange disease, and his wife ran mad?"

Ikenna was perplexed. She continued, "Since the death of Nwosu, the chief priest, strange things have been happening in our land. They blame you for all these calamities."

"Hey, Erinma, this is too much for my cousin Odochi to bear. I am so sorry for all these misfortunes; I must see them."

"I hear you, but I suggest you do not go alone. Remember, the villagers are unhappy with you—even your family members. Ikenna, I strongly believe that God preserved your life for a purpose. He wants to use you to bring about a change in our land. I am happy for you," she added and smiled warmly at him.

He smiled back.

Chapter 10 | The Journey

At Umukam, Ikenna and the Reverend were treating themselves to a salacious meal of abacha and roast fish. Ikenna, who had not been happy since he heard what had happened to his uncle, did not have a big appetite that day.

"Ikenna, why are you not eating your food? Isn't abacha your favorite any longer?"

Ikenna chuckled half-heartedly and replied, "No, Father. I still love Abacha, as always. I'm just bothered about my cousin Odochi and his loss."

"Ikenna, you should cast your cares on the Lord. Everything that happens is predetermined by God. There are no mistakes. You do not have to worry, son. Also, you will not be doing yourself any good by not eating. We are going to face a serious battle in your place; we must equip ourselves with prayers, but we will also need to eat. Food has its place for physical vitality and strength. Okay?"

"Okay, Father."

A downtrodden Ikenna, who had been nursing his abacha all the while, took a few spoonfuls of the meal.

Three days later, the Reverend, Ikenna, and a seminarian were at his place. Obinna, Odochi's elder brother, seeing them from afar, sprang up with pure rage and raced toward him like a lion that had just noticed a prey.

"I cannot believe that you are wicked and heartless, Ikenna. After all that my father did for you and your family, is this how you repay us? Odochi told me, but I didn't believe her until I came back and saw things for myself. How could you?"

Ikenna maintained a calm demeanour. "Obinna, my brother, I am very sure that you know I am not a wicked person. I am forever grateful for what your family did for us. At the same time, I want to let you know that I am a changed man. My life is no longer the same."

"You people blame me for everything. I can no longer understand you people. If this God that delivered me before your very eyes is still alive, Mama will be healed."

"Come, Odochi, where is Mama?"

"You mean our mama? Oh! She is in the small hut in the backyard, the one close to where we rear our native goats."

"Father, let's go and see her."

The Reverend nodded and followed.

When they arrived, Mama Odochi was seen crouching at one end of the hut. Streaks of dirt covered most of her face, and there were several cuts with smears of blood on her body as if she had been wounded with a jagged substance. She was interacting cheerfully with an army of ants. When she noticed them, she looked angry.

"You see?" she told the ants, nudging her head toward the people. "You see what I was talking about? They can never give me privacy. I can never enjoy a moment of solitude."

She turned to the Reverend. "What is wrong with you people? Unu wu nde ara? Are you people mad?"

Obinna muttered words scornfully under his breath and shook his head in dismay. Odochi, with tears trickling down her face, went to calm her down, but Mama Odochi retreated frantically.

"Don't touch me, o! Before you infect me with your madness."

"Odochi, leave her. I will take it from here," the Reverend stepped in.

"That is right! Leave me alone. If you are jealous of my friends, go find your own!" she said, using her hands to cover the insects festering all over her.

While she kept yelling, the Reverend and Ikenna started to pray. About three minutes into the prayer, Mama Odochi, who had been gazing scornfully all the while, hysterically covered her face with her palms and screamed.

"For in Jesus' name, we have prayed. Amen."

Obinna was in a corner, picking his nails indifferently. Odochi knelt at a spot, trying her best not to choke on restrained tears.

Mama Odochi slowly uncovered her face and stared blankly at everyone for a few seconds. The next moment, she wore a frown as if she had regained awareness. Then she turned to Odochi and gave her a puzzled look.

"Odochi, why are you crying?" She turned to Ikenna. "Ikenna? Ikenna, it has been ages since I saw you."

She gazed abruptly at the Reverend, the seminarian, and back at Ikenna. "Who are the visitors? Why is my daughter crying? Someone tell me what is going on here?"

"Mama!" Odochi sprang up with irrepressible joy and embraced her mother. Her mother remained aloof, still filled with utter confusion. Obinna ran toward them and joined the embrace, his eyes brimming with tears.

"Can you guys please tell me what is going on here?"

"Obinna, look! Even her wounds have disappeared!" Odochi said gleefully.

"This is incredible!" Obinna said. Then he stood and turned to the Reverend and Ikenna. "Indeed, you're serving a mighty God. I am deeply grateful. How can I possibly repay you?"

Anyone who heard the news brought their sick ones to be healed, and they were equally led to Christ.

"Ikenna, it's been six months since we came here. I am a missionary; I don't stay too long in one place. Soon, I will be embarking on a journey. This time, you are coming with me."

Ikenna jumped up with boundless joy and embraced the Reverend.

"Thank you! Thank you! Thank you!"

The Reverend chuckled as if expecting that reaction and patted him endearingly.

"Oh, my dear Ikenna, this is ministry; it's highly demanding. You may not understand until you get into the field," the Reverend continued. "These seminarians that came with us are capable of handling the church here. My heart is filled with joy. They are so zealous in the things of God. It is best we leave now to allow room for growth. Remember, a prophet has no honour in his own country."

"Thank you so much, sir! So...where shall we be going?"

"Oh, this time, we shall be going to Osuofia. It's a place I have been before, but I'd like us to revisit the village. Those people were hospitable to me, though quite a number were hostile. All the same, I have a premonition to visit them."

"Father, I did not get what you mean by a prophet has no honour in his own country'?"

"Oh, dear. You see, I don't want you to suffer what I suffered at the hands of my people. In the place I am taking you, you will be going as a missionary, and that will earn you more respect. You will be able to do excellently well with the help of our God."

"So why do you want me to come with you?"

"Ikenna, I respect the call of God upon your life. These people have a similar case to your people. They chose the wrong person as the custodian of their oracle, and strange things have happened to them. This has opened a ministerial door for me. I tried a little while there, but believe you will accomplish more by His grace."

Ikenna nodded approvingly but still wore a puzzled expression.

Two months later, Reverend John and Ikenna were in Osuofia.

"Where are we going to stay, Reverend?" Ikenna asked.

"That is not a problem; let it not bother you. We can stay anywhere. Or are you not the one who slept in the village square some time ago?"

"Sir, I don't want to have that experience again. It was a horrible one."

"Sure! No, it won't happen again. But there is a particular place I'd like us to visit first. The last time I visited, the man's wife was pregnant, so I'm guessing she has given birth by now."

Ikenna nervously pinched his thigh, trying to re-center himself on the tricycle.

"Reverend, these people look hostile. They are not even responding to our greetings. Are you sure things will go smoothly here?"

"Just greet them anyway; it is just a sign of respect. When we get to Odili's family, they will receive us well. Speaking of Odili, there is a market about a mile away from here. I'd like us to buy them gifts—maybe some foodstuffs like garri, bonga fish, okporoko... What do you think?"

"Not bad at all," Ikenna replied distractedly, trying his best to avoid making eye contact with a burly man with bloodshot eyes passing by. He gazed at the antelope lying lifelessly on the man's broad shoulder. It must have suffered a great ordeal.

After about an hour, as they reached Odili's home, a woman's voice stopped them in their tracks.

"Ewoh! Who am I seeing? Reverend?" said Ogechi.

"Ah! Ogechi, how have you been?"

"Fine oh! How are you doing, Reverend?"

"Healthy and hearty. It is so good to see you."

"You just abandoned us."

The Reverend chuckled upon hearing that. "My dear, you know the nature of my work."

"I understand, Father. Anyway, I am happy to see you. You are welcome!"

"Same here! What exactly are you doing by the side of the bush all alone?"

"Reverend, you won't understand. This root that I am cutting is for my baby."

"What do you mean?"

"My baby has refused to come out oh. I am not the only one in this village facing this predicament."

"Hmm! I was actually taken aback by the bulge on your stomach. I was wondering if it was the same pregnancy or another."

"Father, it is the same pregnancy oh."

"Ah, is it not long overdue? What is the problem?"

"The same problems oh... This village has been turned into a chaotic mess." She stopped, then exhaled in dismay. "Only God can help us."

"Don't worry. We are here. God is able to do all things. We were actually going to your house before we met you."

"Ah, what are we waiting for? Let us go home. I was actually rounding off!"

She tried kneeling down to carry her implements, and a whimper escaped her mouth due to the abnormally large protrusion. The Reverend was concerned.

"Ikenna, help her with that." Ikenna did as commanded.

"No, oh! Do not bother. I will do it myself." Ikenna insisted, but she refused. With feigned strength, she put the roots in the sack and carried the tools with her free hand. She heaved heavily and turned to the Reverend with a weary smile. They were genuinely concerned.

"Oya, let us go." She started toward the direction of her home, ignoring their sympathetic looks. The Reverend and Ikenna joined her.

"Papa Ukachi, Papa Ukachi, oh!" she called to her husband several times. Footsteps were heard approaching.

"Mama Ukachi, is that you? I have been looking all over for you. How many times do I have to tell you to stop straining yourself? Where is that woman?"

"I am here, oh! Guess what? The Reverend is here!"

"Reverend! You mean Reverend John?!" He hastened his footsteps, and in no time, he was in the living room. Upon seeing the Reverend, he grinned.

"Ah! The Reverend! We thought we would never see you again. Kedu?"

"I am well, thank you. And yourself?"

"We are good, oh. Despite everything, we keep striving. And who is the lad you are with?"

"Oh, this is Ikenna. He is my spiritual son."

"Is that so?" Odili asked comically.

"Yes," the Reverend and Ikenna chanted at the same time.

Ikenna's face shone with a prideful smile. He greeted, "Good day, sir."

"It is well with you, boy." He turned back to the Reverend. "So you just deserted us, eh, Reverend?"

"I cannot forget in a hurry how you people helped me. Even when those idol worshippers wanted to tear me apart, you saw to my rescue. That is why we are here. God Almighty will use your family to bring blessings to other families. We are going to pray for your wife. After three days, she will carry your baby on her lap."

"Ah!" Ogechi shouted and grabbed her belly. "The baby kicked when you said that!" She jumped up and started to sing and dance as if the baby had already been delivered.

News spread around the village of Osuofia about Ogechi's safe delivery. Other pregnant women rushed to her house to find out how it happened.

"Mama baby, congrats, oh! Could you please tell us what happened?"

"You may not believe me, but that same Reverend that you people chased away some months back came back and prayed for me. He said that I would put to bed in three days' time."

"You do not mean it! Where can I find him?"

"He is not around, but he promised to come back in a week's time to see my baby."

"Ola, why the face?"

"Mama baby, you will not understand. I am tired of carrying this baby; I want to deliver now."

"Trust me, I do understand. Don't worry; he will be back in three days' time."

"Ogechi, are those not the same people who stopped talking to us because we were interacting with the Reverend?" whispered Odili. "I am not sure that he will be willing to pray for them. Fair-weather friends. I will personally chase them away."

The Reverend and Ikenna came back as they had promised. They were so happy to see Ogechi's baby and thanked God.

"Reverend, please, the pregnant women want you to pray for them after they heard my testimony. They have been waiting for you since morning."

"Do you mean that they have been here since morning?"

"Yes, I told them that you would be coming today."

"Wait a minute, who is that woman there? Is it Ola?"

Ola stood shyly among the group of women with abnormal protrusions, avoiding eye contact with the Reverend and gesturing at Ogechi with pleading eyes to intervene for her.

"I can still remember all the things that she did to you. Please forgive her. I am on my knees." Ogechi went down on her knees.

"Please stand up! You don't have to do that. Forgiveness is the first thing I learned as a child of God. You must let go of another's misdeeds. Judgment is of God."

"But my husband is not happy with them. He even threatened to chase them away, but I pleaded with him."

"Yes." Odili sat up, shooting an evil scowl at Ogechi, who bashfully flung her face away. "They are not deserving of—"

"It's okay, Odili, I've forgiven them," the Reverend interrupted.

"Please do to us what you did to her; we want to have our own babies," one of them said. They all started to plead simultaneously.

"We did not do anything special for her. We just prayed for her, and she believed. We are going to pray for all of you, but that would be on one condition: go and call your husbands."

They all scurried away to their various homes in search of their husbands and almost came back at the same time. After they had settled in, the Reverend spoke:

"I decided to call you people here because it takes two to tango. I have listened to your wives, but I have not heard from you. Do you want to see your babies?"

"Yes!"

"Of course!"

"Most definitely," chorused their husbands.

"I understand that the wrath of your god fell on them, which is why they are carrying their babies longer than they should."

"Yes, Reverend, we are afraid because we don't know what will happen next."

"We cannot afford to lose our wives!"

"Before we pray for them, I will tell you the story of this young man. I promise to make it short because it is indeed a very long one. Ikenna was chosen to be the custodian of an oracle in Aguta. He ran away because of his newfound faith in Jesus Christ. Months later, his people found him, took him home, and he renounced their beliefs. It wasn't easy, but my God fought for him. I will tell you the remaining part of the story later. We are going to pray now, and I believe you will have a safe delivery."

They prayed for them and left for Aguta to see how the people were growing in faith.

Three weeks later, they went back to Osuofia. It was a thing of joy when they heard that all the fourteen women had delivered safely, one after the other. These families were grateful and wished they could stay with them.

"Now let me tell you the whole story. We were both bound up, about to be set ablaze. Just like a flash, fire fell from above, untied our ropes, and set Aguba Shrine ablaze. Today, there is a church in his village. I brought him here because I know that if God did it for him in that village, He can do much more in this village."

From that day, many believed in the Almighty God, and things turned around in their favour. Ikenna was ordained a priest. He remained in Osuofia, and God used him mightily.

At Umukam, Ikenna and the Reverend were treating themselves to a salacious meal of abacha and roast fish. Ikenna, who had not been happy since he heard what had happened to his uncle, did not have a big appetite that day.

"Ikenna, why are you not eating your food? Isn't abacha your favorite any longer?"

Ikenna chuckled half-heartedly and replied, "No, Father. I still love Abacha, as always. I'm just bothered about my cousin Odochi and his loss."

"Ikenna, you should cast your cares on the Lord. Everything that happens is predetermined by God. There are no mistakes. You do not have to worry, son. Also, you will not be doing yourself any good by not eating. We are going to face a serious battle in your place; we must equip ourselves with prayers, but we will also need to eat. Food has its place for physical vitality and strength. Okay?"

"Okay, Father."

A downtrodden Ikenna, who had been nursing his abacha all the while, took a few spoonfuls of the meal.

Three days later, the Reverend, Ikenna, and a seminarian were at his place. Obinna, Odochi's elder brother, seeing them from afar, sprang up with pure rage and raced toward him like a lion that had just noticed a prey.

"I cannot believe that you are wicked and heartless, Ikenna. After all that my father did for you and your family, is this how you repay us? Odochi told me, but I didn't believe her until I came back and saw things for myself. How could you?"

Ikenna maintained a calm demeanour. "Obinna, my brother, I am very sure that you know I am not a wicked person. I am forever grateful for what your family did for us. At the same time, I want to let you know that I am a changed man. My life is no longer the same."

"You people blame me for everything. I can no longer understand you people. If this God that delivered me before your very eyes is still alive, Mama will be healed."

"Come, Odochi, where is Mama?"

"You mean our mama? Oh! She is in the small hut in the backyard, the one close to where we rear our native goats."

"Father, let's go and see her."

The Reverend nodded and followed.

When they arrived, Mama Odochi was seen crouching at one end of the hut. Streaks of dirt covered most of her face, and there were several cuts with smears of blood on her body as if she had been wounded with a jagged substance. She was interacting cheerfully with an army of ants. When she noticed them, she looked angry.

"You see?" she told the ants, nudging her head toward the people. "You see what I was talking about? They can never give me privacy. I can never enjoy a moment of solitude."

She turned to the Reverend. "What is wrong with you people? Unu wu nde ara? Are you people mad?"

Obinna muttered words scornfully under his breath and shook his head in dismay. Odochi, with tears trickling down her face, went to calm her down, but Mama Odochi retreated frantically.

"Don't touch me, o! Before you infect me with your madness."

"Odochi, leave her. I will take it from here," the Reverend stepped in.

"That is right! Leave me alone. If you are jealous of my friends, go find your own!" she said, using her hands to cover the insects festering all over her.

While she kept yelling, the Reverend and Ikenna started to pray. About three minutes into the prayer, Mama Odochi, who had been gazing scornfully all the while, hysterically covered her face with her palms and screamed.

"For in Jesus' name, we have prayed. Amen."

Obinna was in a corner, picking his nails indifferently. Odochi knelt at a spot, trying her best not to choke on restrained tears.

Mama Odochi slowly uncovered her face and stared blankly at everyone for a few seconds. The next moment, she wore a frown as if she had regained awareness. Then she turned to Odochi and gave her a puzzled look.

"Odochi, why are you crying?" She turned to Ikenna. "Ikenna? Ikenna, it has been ages since I saw you."

She gazed abruptly at the Reverend, the seminarian, and back at Ikenna. "Who are the visitors? Why is my daughter crying? Someone tell me what is going on here?"

"Mama!" Odochi sprang up with irrepressible joy and embraced her mother. Her mother remained aloof, still filled with utter confusion. Obinna ran toward them and joined the embrace, his eyes brimming with tears.

"Can you guys please tell me what is going on here?"

"Obinna, look! Even her wounds have disappeared!" Odochi said gleefully.

"This is incredible!" Obinna said. Then he stood and turned to the Reverend and Ikenna.

"Indeed, you're serving a mighty God. I am deeply grateful. How can I possibly repay you?"

Anyone who heard the news brought their sick ones to be healed, and they were equally led to Christ.

"Ikenna, it's been six months since we came here. I am a missionary; I don't stay too long in one place. Soon, I will be embarking on a journey. This time, you are coming with me."

Ikenna jumped up with boundless joy and embraced the Reverend.

"Thank you! Thank you! Thank you!"

The Reverend chuckled as if expecting that reaction and patted him endearingly.

"Oh, my dear Ikenna, this is ministry; it's highly demanding. You may not understand until you get into the field," the Reverend continued. "These seminarians that came with us are capable of handling the church here. My heart is filled with joy. They are so zealous in the things of God. It is best we leave now to allow room for growth. Remember, a prophet has no honour in his own country."

"Thank you so much, sir! So...where shall we be going?"

"Oh, this time, we shall be going to Osuofia. It's a place I have been before, but I'd like us to revisit the village. Those people were hospitable to me, though quite a number were hostile. All the same, I have a premonition to visit them."

"Father, I did not get what you mean by a prophet has no honour in his own country'?"

"Oh, dear. You see, I don't want you to suffer what I suffered at the hands of my people. In the place I am taking you, you will be going as a missionary, and that will earn you more respect. You will be able to do excellently well with the help of our God."

"So why do you want me to come with you?"

"Ikenna, I respect the call of God upon your life. These people have a similar case to your people. They chose the wrong person as the custodian of their oracle, and strange things have happened to them. This has opened a ministerial door for me. I tried a little while there, but believe you will accomplish more by His grace."

Ikenna nodded approvingly but still wore a puzzled expression.

Two months later, Reverend John and Ikenna were in Osuofia.

"Where are we going to stay, Reverend?" Ikenna asked.

"That is not a problem; let it not bother you. We can stay anywhere. Or are you not the one who slept in the village square some time ago?"

"Sir, I don't want to have that experience again. It was a horrible one."

"Sure! No, it won't happen again. But there is a particular place I'd like us to visit first. The last time I visited, the man's wife was pregnant, so I'm guessing she has given birth by now."

Ikenna nervously pinched his thigh, trying to re-center himself on the tricycle.

"Reverend, these people look hostile. They are not even responding to our greetings. Are you sure things will go smoothly here?"

"Just greet them anyway; it is just a sign of respect. When we get to Odili's family, they will receive us well. Speaking of Odili, there is a market about a mile away from here. I'd like us to buy them gifts—maybe some foodstuffs like garri, bonga fish, okporoko... What do you think?"

"Not bad at all," Ikenna replied distractedly, trying his best to avoid making eye contact with a burly man with bloodshot eyes passing by. He gazed at the antelope lying lifelessly on the man's broad shoulder. It must have suffered a great ordeal.

After about an hour, as they reached Odili's home, a woman's voice stopped them in their tracks.

"Ewoh! Who am I seeing? Reverend?" said Ogechi.

"Ah! Ogechi, how have you been?"

"Fine oh! How are you doing, Reverend?"

"Healthy and hearty. It is so good to see you."

"You just abandoned us."

The Reverend chuckled upon hearing that. "My dear, you know the nature of my work."

"I understand, Father. Anyway, I am happy to see you. You are welcome!"

"Same here! What exactly are you doing by the side of the bush all alone?"

"Reverend, you won't understand. This root that I am cutting is for my baby."

"What do you mean?"

"My baby has refused to come out oh. I am not the only one in this village facing this predicament."

"Hmm! I was actually taken aback by the bulge on your stomach. I was wondering if it was the same pregnancy or another."

"Father, it is the same pregnancy oh."

"Ah, is it not long overdue? What is the problem?"

"The same problems oh... This village has been turned into a chaotic mess." She stopped, then exhaled in dismay. "Only God can help us."

"Don't worry. We are here. God is able to do all things. We were actually going to your house before we met you."

"Ah, what are we waiting for? Let us go home. I was actually rounding off!"

She tried kneeling down to carry her implements, and a whimper escaped her mouth due to the abnormally large protrusion. The Reverend was concerned.

"Ikenna, help her with that." Ikenna did as commanded.

"No, oh! Do not bother. I will do it myself." Ikenna insisted, but she refused. With feigned strength, she put the roots in the sack and carried the tools with her free hand. She heaved heavily and turned to the Reverend with a weary smile. They were genuinely concerned.

"Oya, let us go." She started toward the direction of her home, ignoring their sympathetic looks. The Reverend and Ikenna joined her.

"Papa Ukachi, Papa Ukachi, oh!" she called to her husband several times. Footsteps were heard approaching.

"Mama Ukachi, is that you? I have been looking all over for you. How many times do I have to tell you to stop straining yourself? Where is that woman?"

"I am here, oh! Guess what? The Reverend is here!"

"Reverend! You mean Reverend John?!" He hastened his footsteps, and in no time, he was in the living room. Upon seeing the Reverend, he grinned.

"Ah! The Reverend! We thought we would never see you again. Kedu?"

"I am well, thank you. And yourself?"

"We are good, oh. Despite everything, we keep striving. And who is the lad you are with?"

"Oh, this is Ikenna. He is my spiritual son."

"Is that so?" Odili asked comically.

"Yes," the Reverend and Ikenna chanted at the same time.

Ikenna's face shone with a prideful smile. He greeted, "Good day, sir."

"It is well with you, boy." He turned back to the Reverend. "So you just deserted us, eh, Reverend?"

"I cannot forget in a hurry how you people helped me. Even when those idol worshippers wanted to tear me apart, you saw to my rescue. That is why we are here. God Almighty will use your family to bring blessings to other families. We are going to pray for your wife. After three days, she will carry your baby on her lap."

"Ah!" Ogechi shouted and grabbed her belly. "The baby kicked when you said that!" She jumped up and started to sing and dance as if the baby had already been delivered.

News spread around the village of Osuofia about Ogechi's safe delivery. Other pregnant women rushed to her house to find out how it happened.

"Mama baby, congrats, oh! Could you please tell us what happened?"

"You may not believe me, but that same Reverend that you people chased away some months back came back and prayed for me. He said that I would put to bed in three days' time."

"You do not mean it! Where can I find him?"

"He is not around, but he promised to come back in a week's time to see my baby."

"Ola, why the face?"

"Mama baby, you will not understand. I am tired of carrying this baby; I want to deliver now."

"Trust me, I do understand. Don't worry; he will be back in three days' time."

"Ogechi, are those not the same people who stopped talking to us because we were interacting with the Reverend?" whispered Odili. "I am not sure that he will be willing to pray for them. Fair-weather friends. I will personally chase them away."

The Reverend and Ikenna came back as they had promised. They were so happy to see Ogechi's baby and thanked God.

"Reverend, please, the pregnant women want you to pray for them after they heard my testimony. They have been waiting for you since morning."

"Do you mean that they have been here since morning?"

"Yes, I told them that you would be coming today."

"Wait a minute, who is that woman there? Is it Ola?"

Ola stood shyly among the group of women with abnormal protrusions, avoiding eye contact with the

Reverend and gesturing at Ogechi with pleading eyes to intervene for her.

"I can still remember all the things that she did to you. Please forgive her. I am on my knees." Ogechi went down on her knees.

"Please stand up! You don't have to do that. Forgiveness is the first thing I learned as a child of God. You must let go of another's misdeeds. Judgment is of God."

"But my husband is not happy with them. He even threatened to chase them away, but I pleaded with him."

"Yes." Odili sat up, shooting an evil scowl at Ogechi, who bashfully flung her face away. "They are not deserving of—"

"It's okay, Odili, I've forgiven them," the Reverend interrupted.

"Please do to us what you did to her; we want to have our own babies," one of them said. They all started to plead simultaneously.

"We did not do anything special for her. We just prayed for her, and she believed. We are going to pray for all of you, but that would be on one condition: go and call your husbands."

They all scurried away to their various homes in search of their husbands and almost came back at the same time. After they had settled in, the Reverend spoke:

"I decided to call you people here because it takes two to tango. I have listened to your wives, but I have not heard from you. Do you want to see your babies?"

"Yes!"

"Of course!"

"Most definitely," chorused their husbands.

"I understand that the wrath of your god fell on them, which is why they are carrying their babies longer than they should."

"Yes, Reverend, we are afraid because we don't know what will happen next."

"We cannot afford to lose our wives!"

"Before we pray for them, I will tell you the story of this young man. I promise to make it short because it is indeed a very long one. Ikenna was chosen to be the custodian of an oracle in Aguta. He ran away because of his newfound faith in Jesus Christ. Months later, his people found him, took him home, and he renounced their beliefs. It wasn't easy, but my God fought for him. I will tell you the remaining part of the story later. We are going to pray now, and I believe you will have a safe delivery."

They prayed for them and left for Aguta to see how the people were growing in faith.

Three weeks later, they went back to Osuofia. It was a thing of joy when they heard that all the fourteen women had delivered safely, one after the other. These families were grateful and wished they could stay with them.

"Now let me tell you the whole story. We were both bound up, about to be set ablaze. Just like a flash, fire fell from above, untied our ropes, and set Aguba Shrine ablaze. Today, there is a church in his village. I brought him here because I know that if God did it for him in that village, He can do much more in this village."

From that day, many believed in the Almighty God, and things turned around in their favour. Ikenna was ordained a priest. He remained in Osuofia, and God used him mightily.

At Umukam, Ikenna and the Reverend were treating themselves to a salacious meal of abacha and roast fish. Ikenna, who had not been happy since he heard what had happened to his uncle, did not have a big appetite that day.

"Ikenna, why are you not eating your food? Isn't abacha your favorite any longer?"

Ikenna chuckled half-heartedly and replied, "No, Father. I still love Abacha, as always. I'm just bothered about my cousin Odochi and his loss."

"Ikenna, you should cast your cares on the Lord. Everything that happens is predetermined by God. There are no mistakes. You do not have to worry, son. Also, you will not be doing yourself any good by not eating. We are going to face a serious battle in your place; we must equip ourselves with prayers, but we will also need to eat. Food has its place for physical vitality and strength. Okay?"

"Okay, Father."

A downtrodden Ikenna, who had been nursing his abacha all the while, took a few spoonfuls of the meal.

Three days later, the Reverend, Ikenna, and a seminarian were at his place. Obinna, Odochi's elder brother, seeing them from afar, sprang up with pure rage and raced toward him like a lion that had just noticed a prey.

"I cannot believe that you are wicked and heartless, Ikenna. After all that my father did for you and your family, is this how you repay us? Odochi told me, but I didn't believe her until I came back and saw things for myself. How could you?"

Ikenna maintained a calm demeanour. "Obinna, my brother, I am very sure that you know I am not a wicked person. I am forever grateful for what your family did for us. At the same time, I want to let you know that I am a changed man. My life is no longer the same."

"You people blame me for everything. I can no longer understand you people. If this God that delivered me before your very eyes is still alive, Mama will be healed."

"Come, Odochi, where is Mama?"

"You mean our mama? Oh! She is in the small hut in the backyard, the one close to where we rear our native goats."

"Father, let's go and see her."

The Reverend nodded and followed.

When they arrived, Mama Odochi was seen crouching at one end of the hut. Streaks of dirt covered most of her face, and there were several cuts with smears of blood on her body as if she had been wounded with a jagged substance. She was interacting cheerfully with an army of ants. When she noticed them, she looked angry.

"You see?" she told the ants, nudging her head toward the people. "You see what I was talking about? They can never give me privacy. I can never enjoy a moment of solitude."

She turned to the Reverend. "What is wrong with you people? Unu wu nde ara? Are you people mad?"

Obinna muttered words scornfully under his breath and shook his head in dismay. Odochi, with tears trickling down her face, went to calm her down, but Mama Odochi retreated frantically.

"Don't touch me, o! Before you infect me with your madness."

"Odochi, leave her. I will take it from here," the Reverend stepped in.

"That is right! Leave me alone. If you are jealous of my friends, go find your own!" she said, using her hands to cover the insects festering all over her.

While she kept yelling, the Reverend and Ikenna started to pray. About three minutes into the prayer, Mama Odochi, who had been gazing scornfully all the while, hysterically covered her face with her palms and screamed.

"For in Jesus' name, we have prayed. Amen."

Obinna was in a corner, picking his nails indifferently. Odochi knelt at a spot, trying her best not to choke on restrained tears.

Mama Odochi slowly uncovered her face and stared blankly at everyone for a few seconds. The next moment, she wore a frown as if she had regained awareness. Then she turned to Odochi and gave her a puzzled look.

"Odochi, why are you crying?" She turned to Ikenna. "Ikenna? Ikenna, it has been ages since I saw you."

She gazed abruptly at the Reverend, the seminarian, and back at Ikenna. "Who are the visitors? Why is my daughter crying? Someone tell me what is going on here?"

"Mama!" Odochi sprang up with irrepressible joy and embraced her mother. Her mother remained aloof, still filled with utter confusion. Obinna ran toward them and joined the embrace, his eyes brimming with tears.

"Can you guys please tell me what is going on here?"

"Obinna, look! Even her wounds have disappeared!" Odochi said gleefully.

"This is incredible!" Obinna said. Then he stood and turned to the Reverend and Ikenna.

"Indeed, you're serving a mighty God. I am deeply grateful. How can I possibly repay you?"

Anyone who heard the news brought their sick ones to be healed, and they were equally led to Christ.

"Ikenna, it's been six months since we came here. I am a missionary; I don't stay too long in one place. Soon, I will be embarking on a journey. This time, you are coming with me."

Ikenna jumped up with boundless joy and embraced the Reverend.

"Thank you! Thank you! Thank you!"

The Reverend chuckled as if expecting that reaction and patted him endearingly.

"Oh, my dear Ikenna, this is ministry; it's highly demanding. You may not understand until you get into the field," the Reverend continued. "These seminarians that came with us are capable of handling the church here. My heart is filled with joy. They are so zealous in the things of God. It is best we leave now to allow room for growth. Remember, a prophet has no honour in his own country."

"Thank you so much, sir! So...where shall we be going?"

"Oh, this time, we shall be going to Osuofia. It's a place I have been before, but I'd like us to revisit the village. Those people were hospitable to me, though quite a number were hostile. All the same, I have a premonition to visit them."

"Father, I did not get what you mean by a prophet has no honour in his own country'?"

"Oh, dear. You see, I don't want you to suffer what I suffered at the hands of my people. In the place I am taking you, you will be going as a missionary, and that will earn you more respect.

You will be able to do excellently well with the help of our God."

"So why do you want me to come with you?"

"Ikenna, I respect the call of God upon your life. These people have a similar case to your people. They chose the wrong person as the custodian of their oracle, and strange things have happened to them. This has opened a ministerial door for me. I tried a little while there, but believe you will accomplish more by His grace."

Ikenna nodded approvingly but still wore a puzzled expression.

Two months later, Reverend John and Ikenna were in Osuofia.

"Where are we going to stay, Reverend?" Ikenna asked.

"That is not a problem; let it not bother you. We can stay anywhere. Or are you not the one who slept in the village square some time ago?"

"Sir, I don't want to have that experience again. It was a horrible one."

"Sure! No, it won't happen again. But there is a particular place I'd like us to visit first. The last time I visited, the man's wife was pregnant, so I'm guessing she has given birth by now."

Ikenna nervously pinched his thigh, trying to re-center himself on the tricycle.

"Reverend, these people look hostile. They are not even responding to our greetings. Are you sure things will go smoothly here?"

"Just greet them anyway; it is just a sign of respect. When we get to Odili's family, they will receive us well. Speaking of Odili, there is a market about a mile away from here. I'd like us to buy them gifts—maybe some foodstuffs like garri, bonga fish, okporoko... What do you think?"

"Not bad at all," Ikenna replied distractedly, trying his best to avoid making eye contact with a burly man with bloodshot eyes passing by. He gazed at the antelope lying lifelessly on the man's broad shoulder. It must have suffered a great ordeal.

After about an hour, as they reached Odili's home, a woman's voice stopped them in their tracks.

"Ewoh! Who am I seeing? Reverend?" said Ogechi.

"Ah! Ogechi, how have you been?"

"Fine oh! How are you doing, Reverend?"

"Healthy and hearty. It is so good to see you."

"You just abandoned us."

The Reverend chuckled upon hearing that. "My dear, you know the nature of my work."

"I understand, Father. Anyway, I am happy to see you. You are welcome!"

"Same here! What exactly are you doing by the side of the bush all alone?"

"Reverend, you won't understand. This root that I am cutting is for my baby."

"What do you mean?"

"My baby has refused to come out oh. I am not the only one in this village facing this predicament."

"Hmm! I was actually taken aback by the bulge on your stomach. I was wondering if it was the same pregnancy or another."

"Father, it is the same pregnancy oh."

"Ah, is it not long overdue? What is the problem?"

"The same problems oh... This village has been turned into a chaotic mess." She stopped, then exhaled in dismay. "Only God can help us."

"Don't worry. We are here. God is able to do all things. We were actually going to your house before we met you."

"Ah, what are we waiting for? Let us go home. I was actually rounding off!"

She tried kneeling down to carry her implements, and a whimper escaped her mouth due to the abnormally large protrusion. The Reverend was concerned.

"Ikenna, help her with that." Ikenna did as commanded.

"No, oh! Do not bother. I will do it myself." Ikenna insisted, but she refused. With feigned strength, she put the roots in the sack and carried the tools with her free hand. She heaved heavily and turned to the Reverend with a weary smile. They were genuinely concerned.

"Oya, let us go." She started toward the direction of her home, ignoring their sympathetic looks. The Reverend and Ikenna joined her.

"Papa Ukachi, Papa Ukachi, oh!" she called to her husband several times. Footsteps were heard approaching.

"Mama Ukachi, is that you? I have been looking all over for you. How many times do I have to tell you to stop straining yourself? Where is that woman?"

"I am here, oh! Guess what? The Reverend is here!"

"Reverend! You mean Reverend John?!" He hastened his footsteps, and in no time, he was in the living room. Upon seeing the Reverend, he grinned.

"Ah! The Reverend! We thought we would never see you again. Kedu?"

"I am well, thank you. And yourself?"

"We are good, oh. Despite everything, we keep striving. And who is the lad you are with?"

"Oh, this is Ikenna. He is my spiritual son."

"Is that so?" Odili asked comically.

"Yes," the Reverend and Ikenna chanted at the same time.

Ikenna's face shone with a prideful smile. He greeted, "Good day, sir."

"It is well with you, boy." He turned back to the Reverend. "So you just deserted us, eh, Reverend?"

"I cannot forget in a hurry how you people helped me. Even when those idol worshippers wanted to tear me apart, you saw to my rescue. That is why we are here. God Almighty will use your family to bring blessings to other families. We are going to pray for your wife. After three days, she will carry your baby on her lap."

"Ah!" Ogechi shouted and grabbed her belly. "The baby kicked when you said that!" She jumped up and started to sing and dance as if the baby had already been delivered.

News spread around the village of Osuofia about Ogechi's safe delivery. Other pregnant women rushed to her house to find out how it happened.

"Mama baby, congrats, oh! Could you please tell us what happened?"

"You may not believe me, but that same Reverend that you people chased away some months back came back and prayed for me. He said that I would put to bed in three days' time."

"You do not mean it! Where can I find him?"

"He is not around, but he promised to come back in a week's time to see my baby."

"Ola, why the face?"

"Mama baby, you will not understand. I am tired of carrying this baby; I want to deliver now."

"Trust me, I do understand. Don't worry; he will be back in three days' time."

"Ogechi, are those not the same people who stopped talking to us because we were interacting with the Reverend?" whispered Odili. "I am not sure that he will be willing to pray for them. Fair-weather friends. I will personally chase them away."

The Reverend and Ikenna came back as they had promised. They were so happy to see Ogechi's baby and thanked God.

"Reverend, please, the pregnant women want you to pray for them after they heard my testimony. They have been waiting for you since morning."

"Do you mean that they have been here since morning?"

"Yes, I told them that you would be coming today."

"Wait a minute, who is that woman there? Is it Ola?"

Ola stood shyly among the group of women with abnormal protrusions, avoiding eye contact with the Reverend and gesturing at Ogechi with pleading eyes to intervene for her.

"I can still remember all the things that she did to you. Please forgive her. I am on my knees." Ogechi went down on her knees.

"Please stand up! You don't have to do that. Forgiveness is the first thing I learned as a child of God. You must let go of another's misdeeds. Judgment is of God."

"But my husband is not happy with them. He even threatened to chase them away, but I pleaded with him."

"Yes." Odili sat up, shooting an evil scowl at Ogechi, who bashfully flung her face away. "They are not deserving of—"

"It's okay, Odili, I've forgiven them," the Reverend interrupted.

"Please do to us what you did to her; we want to have our own babies," one of them said. They all started to plead simultaneously.

"We did not do anything special for her. We just prayed for her, and she believed. We are going to pray for all of you, but that would be on one condition: go and call your husbands."

They all scurried away to their various homes in search of their husbands and almost came back at the same time. After they had settled in, the Reverend spoke:

"I decided to call you people here because it takes two to tango. I have listened to your wives, but I have not heard from you. Do you want to see your babies?"

"Yes!"

"Of course!"

"Most definitely," chorused their husbands.

"I understand that the wrath of your god fell on them, which is why they are carrying their babies longer than they should."

"Yes, Reverend, we are afraid because we don't know what will happen next."

"We cannot afford to lose our wives!"

"Before we pray for them, I will tell you the story of this young man. I promise to make it short because it is indeed a very long one. Ikenna was chosen to be the custodian of an oracle in Aguta. He ran away because of his newfound faith in Jesus Christ. Months later, his people found him, took him home, and he renounced their beliefs. It wasn't easy, but my God fought for him. I will tell you the remaining part of the story later. We are going to pray now, and I believe you will have a safe delivery."

They prayed for them and left for Aguta to see how the people were growing in faith.

Three weeks later, they went back to Osuofia. It was a thing of joy when they heard that all the fourteen women had delivered safely, one after the other. These families were grateful and wished they could stay with them.

"Now let me tell you the whole story. We were both bound up, about to be set ablaze. Just like a flash, fire fell from above, untied our ropes, and set Aguba Shrine ablaze. Today, there is a church in his village. I brought him here because I know that if God did it for him in that village, He can do much more in this village."

From that day, many believed in the Almighty God, and things turned around in their favour. Ikenna was ordained a priest. He remained in Osuofia, and God used him mightily.